Leopold & Brink: The New Angels

By Chris Fink

Leopold & Brink is a work of fiction. Names, characters, places, and incidents are set in the near future so are the product of the author's imagination, or are used fictitiously. Any resemblance to actual persons, living or dead, is entirely coincidental.

2025 Son of Barton Paperback Edition 1st Print

Published in the United States by Son of Barton, California

ISBN 978-1-930281-99-8

www.studylab.com

You may forget but let me tell you this:
Someone in some future time will think of us.

- Sappho

TABLE OF CONTENTS

The patriarchy is not rule by men.

It is rule by The Masculine, that dangerous fuel that lives in all of us.

This is the story of the end of patriarchy.

1 – SNIPS OF SNAILS

The baby climbed down the mesquite tree with a carefully chosen footful of thorny branches. She stacked them neatly beside the A-frame house she was building. A large snail climbed the hardback book cover she used for the foundation. She'd never seen a snail before. She loved how it moved its antennae in crazed independent twists but could tell it still looked at her. She tried to coax the snail onto her finger and giggled when it retreated into its shell. She tickled its foot, which still peeked out, gripping. She was thrilled by the sticky, sandy softness of it. She gently tapped the shell, a quiet knock, then followed the spiral with her finger. She leaned in close to smell it. This drew the attention of her mother, who was moving about the yard from one chore to another. Semele came over, thinking her toddler had put something inappropriate in her mouth. The girl got very excited, reached out to grab her mother's pant leg firmly, smiled and pointed at her new friend. Her mother crouched down, looked it over, smiled at them both, then picked up the snail. She lifted her daughter into her other arm, and danced the snail through the air as if it were a magical jewel. The girl squealed with joy.

They moved through the house to the kitchen, all the while the mother sing-songingly explaining to her daughter how simple it was to learn from a snail. She sat her joyful girl down and with a swift smack on the granite countertop, she cracked the snail's shell and began peeling it away from its body. The girl went still. Her throat seized, her pulse slowed. Everything went bright and hot. Her mother spoke excitedly about the beauty of the electric simplicity of life as she cut into the creature and pinned its squirming body to a wooden cutting board. The girl felt every subtle poke and caress as her mother dragged aside the heart, kidney, lungs, and other unrelated organs, to expose the ganglia in its animated head, its tentacles still looking at the girl, groping for meaning.

2 – THE MEASURE OF MAN

Brink struggled to keep Leopold's body above water. It felt like he weighed more here.

She expected to see a coastline nearby, but it was endless sea in every direction except the one full of thrusting arms and hardwood poles.

She grabbed one and a few grunting, heroic moments later they were on the deck of a ship at sunset surrounded by golden-brown men who looked at them as if they were idiots. Gazing past their muscled shoulders, the coast was now clear.

One of the sailors crouched next to the immobile Leopold, smacked his face brightly, and leaned in to feel for breath. Another bellowed at Brink, "What are you doing out here, woman?"

"We were swept out by currents," she said, excited that she understood his tricky regional accent. "Our nets were full."

There was silence. The sloshing of waves against the ship's hull became an eerie, shallow breathing. All of the men gathered and stared. There probably wasn't any fishing around here this time of year, her own accent must be terrible, and there was a war on with the neighbors; they'd found a foreigner, female, inexplicably at sea, with an apparently dead local. Whoops, she thought, hiding her joy at things becoming this chaotic so early in the trip.

They shouted mostly incomprehensible slang – mean, sexist stuff she hadn't come across in her extensive study of the period.

She listened patiently, trying to figure out whom she was dealing with and what had gone wrong, until one grabbed her hood and a handful of hair, another her underarm. They tried to drag her over the edge of the boat, but she threw them off like annoying kid brothers.

She took the largest by his shoulders, dug her fingers into the muscles of his broad back, and brought him to his knees. He strained to keep from crying out. The rest backed away, aghast and fascinated. She took a moment, her first moment to look around in awe at the web of worn ropes, the shocked look on the face of the dutiful, salty-bearded helmsman, the smell of the moist winter air, the feel of the thick skin and sweat of the man in her grip, before releasing him. He tumbled onto his face, arms useless. The others helped him retreat.

Their confusion turned to fear. A new look on their faces, as if they were watching, after being lost at sea for years, an island paradise melt under an erupting volcano. Brink couldn't fathom what struck them so deeply until she felt the wind on her wet hair. Her hood, loosened by the effort, had fallen to her neck, exposing her chimeric face and muted purple hair.

She slowly lifted up calming hands and said in her best fifth-century Greek, "Easy, boys. I'm just a girl."

They skittered about like a legislation of baboons.

"I know what she is," said one, comforting them with categorization, "She is a goddess of Libya!"

Brink was bummed. She wasn't surprised they were familiar with the animal hybrid gods of the kingdoms to the south, but it was exactly what she'd hope to avoid, her looks mucking up the adventure so soon after it had begun. She played along to facilitate her and Leopold's departure.

"I'm here to protect this Athenian boy. Really. I will cause no more trouble if you leave us alone," she said. "Any chance for a ride back to Piraeus?"

Power calculations lit their wild eyes. This goddess was strong, they thought, but not large, and jovial, therefore weak, but weak enough to be overcome?

Brink left them to their scheming and crouched beside the not-yet-conscious Leopold, lifting him into her arms. She stepped up on the ship's low railing and prepared to jump back in the water, taking a moment to appreciate the scene, the swaying ship, the absence of any mechanical sound, the wind pushing favorably across the large square sail above them, when a voice wailed across the ship, "My master demands to know the cause of this violent flopping about."

A short triangle of a man in a flowing peach gown approached, took one look at Brink, turned calmly, and returned below deck.

Brink looked back at the men. "I'd love to stay and play," she said, "but I can see we're imposing. I can't decide which one of you I love the most. My blessing shall go to –" She bent at the knee, once again preparing to leap, when the stout man reappeared, imploring her to wait. He was helping an old man up creaking steps.

"Do you understand me?" the old man called across the ship, his voice like an exhausted but loving father.

5

"My dialect will frustrate you," Brink said, keeping an eye on the sailors.

"What is your mother tongue?" the old man said, moving confidently across the deck.

"It's distant. Far, far to the west. Like way over there," she said, extending her long arm towards the setting sun.

"I've traveled great distances, but I've never seen a woman with a beauty like yours."

Brink hoped she'd translated that correctly.

"May we help your companion?" he asked, examining Leopold.

"He is dead," shouted one of the crew, accusingly.

"Is this true?" the old man asked with concern.

"He's fine," said Brink. "He has faint breath, and he can sleep through anything."

"You cannot trust her," another added. "She is a foreign god, stronger than all of us." The man's companions gave him dirty looks.

"Is this true?" the old man asked her politely.

"Yes," she said cracking her fingers in their direction. "I am indeed stronger than all of them."

The sailors made more disapproving sounds. The old man glared at them. "Have you tried to sneak her on for some purpose I would not approve?" he said.

The allegation caused a moment of doubt as the men looked at each other trying to remember who brought her aboard. Brink wondered if this was a cue for her to make a break for it, but there were too many unanswered questions. She and Leopold were supposed to be in open water close to shore at a time when sea travel was rare. That they would appear directly in a ship's path, and one belonging to a non-military fellow like this, was troubling.

"Let's get some dry clothing for you both," said the old man.

The servant was quiet. He was a watcher. Over the years he'd been with his master, he'd also become a thinker, and relished the skills he'd inherited: analyzing expressions, how bodies moved, the words a man chose, the words a woman chose, and what may come next in any situation. Though he couldn't read Brink's intentions or state of mind, he knew she would stay.

And she did.

The old man's caregiver walked back to the stern and started back down the steep steps, gesturing for Brink to follow.

The tiny cabin was adorned with books, a hanging plant, a species Brink was shocked to find she couldn't recognize, an ornate chest, a rich man's modest quarters on a relatively modest yacht. A thin hammock filed with warm furs hung folded against a wall. The rest of the ship at this level contained seating for absent rowers, unemployed during winter. The servant produced a violet wool chiton from a large chest and handed the neatly folded fabric to Brink, who accepted the comfy cloth giddily. He pulled out a deep purple himation of much heavier fabric for Leopold. The evening was becoming chilly.

"If you need help with the pins, I am Diphon. I will be just above," he said, involuntarily scrunching his nose on his way out.

Brink smiled broadly.

She turned and sat quietly for a moment, closed her eyes, and breathed deeply.

She changed Leopold's clothes and put him flat on a soft, flame-colored rug. She studied his silent expression and tried to keep herself from getting emotional. A lapse in her concentration could be disastrous for him at this point. She kissed his cheek and pressed her face against his, then went back up to find the old man lounging in a patio at the end of the long, thin ship. He invited her to sit. The seamen zigzagged along the coast against a counter-wind, shooting occasional dirty looks Brink's way.

"Would you like some wine?"

"Good lord, yes," Brink cried, in English.

"That is your language?" he asked, shocked and half-smiling like a child hearing a balloon pop for the first time.

She corrected herself and returned to Greek, "I'm sorry, I would love to have some wine. I was excited by your question."

"That I could tell, but what a deliberate tongue. Give me more."

"Are you aware of the tribes far north and west. Barbarians? Not barbarians," she struggled, that word meaning any non-Greek.

"We are surrounded by foreigners, child. I am one myself, but I believe you refer to a people well beyond my travels. If you tell me you are Hyperborean, I will not be entirely surprised and will do a happy dance for you."

"Then I am definitely from Hyperborea," she said, waiting anxiously. The old man twitched his heavy eyebrows and spit out a seed. "I sometimes wish my world was magical. Where I come from is all too real. And my language is a combination of many other languages over a long period of violent nonsense," she said, taking a long sip.

The wine was tasty, weirdly sweet, less watered down than Brink expected.

"I'm afraid I will be unable to redirect our voyage. If you need to return to the great city, I can insist they put into shore where it is safe for you to travel back before we get too far away."

"Where are you headed?" Brink asked.

"A long, convoluted journey, I'm afraid. Back to my home in Abdera to gather what is left of my life there, then on to what is left of my life in Sicily, closer, I imagine, to where you are from."

"Moving is always such a hassle," Brink said.

The old man laughed again. He leaned close to her and took her hand. She became flushed. His hand was warm and strong. She laughed at herself, her behavior surprising to both of them.

"What happened to you, dear? What sort of slippery fish have we caught?"

She poured herself some more wine.

The man's face was impossibly kind and deep. Brink fought the urge to figure out who he was by cheating. She was sure neither her educational background nor her preparation for this journey was going to help much with this mystery.

"May I touch your face?" the man asked, surprising Brink.

"Curious. Yes you may."

"You share openly but cannot find anyone who understands. This is familiar to me," he said, his fingertips brushing the outward curve of her face faintly.

She felt paralyzed with bliss. His hands were inside her head, carefully cushioning her from worry.

Something must be wrong, she thought. There's no way this was a coincidence, but the attention she could give to analysis showed nothing strange. Everything was smooth sailing.

The man sat back, sensing Brink was distant. "Now you must tell me," he said, "what *were* you up to in the brisk water?"

"That is my son," she said. "We had a terrible fight with his father and he dumped us in the sea. It is fortunate you came along.

The old man listened quietly.

"I wanted to attend the Lenaia, but he wouldn't allow it. When I insisted and insulted him, he paddled us from our home in Corinth and told me to enjoy the show, pushing us from the boat very far from shore. My son grew exhausted keeping me and my heavy bottom afloat. When he passed out, I kept us up the best I could and then you miraculously arrived."

He listened politely, leaned forward, and took hold of her hand. She could tell he knew she was lying, but she couldn't tell how. That pleased her greatly.

"That is the truth. A wildly contorted version, but a truth. I swear."

"Men can be problematic to women like you. I understand," he quietly replied.

"Wow, you are at least as slippery as me," Brink said.

"Truth, like the sea, is more than its turbulent surface," said the old man.

"Hold on," Brink said, circling back. "Problematic because of my strength? Looks? Or narrative manipulation?"

The old man laughed and clapped, dropping Brink's hand. The separation felt like losing a comfy blanket. She had to look more closely at what was going on so she checked out of the conversation, keeping her countenance attuned enough to appear attentive, which, due to the highly intuitive nature of her host, was likely failing. He went on for some time about the way things were changing politically, a historical summation of the agonizing collapse of an empire that didn't know it was collapsing. Brink found it hard not to listen carefully to his words as she worked. She almost didn't catch when he asked a question.

"I made my living from trying to show truth in the shadows of language," he said. "That is why *I* am on this boat, a boat I once owned, that I've traded my life for. Athens' current wisdom has decided my investigations antagonize her faith. Having been exiled from the great city on the charge of questioning the role of the gods in the affairs of men, I must ask if you are proof of my foolishness."

"You're asking if I'm of Olympus?" Brink said, fully returning to the conversation.

"Or a related elsewhere."

"I am from the same world as you. I promise," said Brink.

"Yes, I know."

"You look disappointed."

"I am disappointed that I'd hoped you'd answer otherwise," said the old man. "For years I've imagined a rich history of our world, our birth not from divinity but from slow natural forces and that that story could capture the imagination as profoundly as the tales of our heroes. But I am as eager for you to be magical as much as any child."

"I can change my answer."

The old man leaned over, put his hand on Brink's forehead, then kissed his hand.

"I could go on were I a younger man, but I must retire for a few hours at least. The safest place for you to disembark would be the eastern coast which we will see tomorrow."

"You sail at night?"

"This is an unconventional journey. You are welcome to share my bed, though it is small and may be a discomfort. Your companion is quite safe where he is."

"I can't pass up a night staring at these stars," Brink said.

"It can get very cold."

"I thought you were too tired," she said, teasing.

"I am far too old and snore much too loud, young lady," he said as he disappeared below.

She laid back and stretched her long arms towards the sleepy moon. She tracked the progress of the boat not by stars but by the heroes, monsters, and gods painted in pinpoints across the black canvas.

She closed her eyes, half snoozing. That this man's dream was identical to her own mother's made Brink worried for the stability of the simulation.

The next moment she was blind, bound, and moving. With slick precision, the men, waiting nearby in silence, rolled her into a heavy net and knocked her over the side in one swift move. They watched her sink and made a prayer to the god of the sea, his glorious temple moonlit on the nearby Sounion coast.

3 – SHAVE AND A HAIRCUT

Taer stood over the four-year-old with an electric razor. The girl was angry, not from being teased about her fur, but the buzzing sound would interrupt her mother's violin playing if she dared turn it on. Taer teased the girl relentlessly about her fur, which had gotten thick and dark. Her mother, sitting on the couch across from her, found it hard to stifle a laugh from this routine.

"You're sure you're not too hot?" Taer said, winking at Semi.

Games like these would often end with the girl running into the other room to the safe arms of Arjun, who would throw her on his shoulders and charge back into the room so she could attack from a better vantage.

Arjun was particularly fond of the youngest of the three women he lived with. He would take her everywhere, showing her off throughout their census-designated place, more a research facility than a town, in Arizona's high desert. He and Semele had been together through every miscarriage. It wasn't until the successful pregnancy when Taer entered their lives, at first a business liaison for the so-called investors.

At two, the girl confidently recognized the family as if her mom had two separate mates living in one house and said as much to neighbors. It made everyone uncomfortable in equal measure. The girl also noticed the nature of those connections had wildly different feels, one more primal, one gentle.

Taer was young and strong and ambitious and full of shoulders. They met in the business meeting where Semele told her investors she was retiring to spend more time with her daughter, even though, unknown to them, her daughter was the direct result of their investment. Taer convinced them that she'd get Semele to come around and finish the work, but she fell in love and moved in shortly after.

Arjun was a family lawyer who commuted south to Phoenix every day but returned home most nights.

Almost every night, the girl would fall asleep with her mother at her upright piano, trying to soften her low voice with a lullaby about the deep forest, the early fields, the bright beautiful sun, and how her little girl was "Princess of the Rezofft Madanadani."

Semele was embarrassed to find she wasn't prepared when the girl, who had learned to speak far sooner than she'd imagined, asked about her own origins, about fatherhood, about how she and her mother connected to the world. In response, Semele taught her to read.

Semele pointed at the long wall of books.

"I want you to imagine pulling a book from the shelf in your mind, opening it, and telling me what's inside," her mother said.

It inspired the girl to read as many as she could and it wasn't long before the library covered every wall. Semele pushed her to connect the books in her mind, to draw a map of their intersecting ideas, nonfiction and fiction alike.

Semele sat in the den with her daughter in her lap. She took three of her daughter's favorite books off the shelf and put them on the floor.

"Remember when you asked me where you came from? The animal we are has been wrestling with that question for a very long time. It's a personal question and it's a uniting question. And the answers are stories. In one, we were created in a great mound and crawled through a long, dark cave into daylight. In one, a Rainbow Serpent slept underground with all living things inside her belly. When the time was right, she vomited them up along with all the bits of the world. There's one with a land of fog and ice melted by fire giants. When the ice dripped, it formed a giant whose children killed him. The earth was made from his flesh and the sea from his blood. Another tells of coming from nothing. One from utter chaos. The Diné up north believe the first world was an island floating in the middle of four seas and there were four more worlds and we're in the fifth one now."

Semele lifted the three books off the floor, handed them to her daughter and told her to stack them in any order. The girl did so. Semele then said to stack them in a different order. The girl did so. Afterward, she picked up the books and put them back on their shelves. She pulled her daughter back into her lap.

"Now tell me what happened with those books," she said.

The girl began recounting the stories found inside each, but her mother stopped her. The girl was confused. She told her to try again and the girl complied, each time trying to synthesize something interesting from her memory of the readings. Her mother kept stopping her. Finally, the girl started from the beginning. "You gave me this one and then this one then this one. And said stack them and I stacked them," she said, grabbing the books from their shelves. She had to pause to remember the order she stacked them, but eventually recreated the event.

"Are you sure you didn't put Mead on top of the Milne?" Semele said as she rearranged the books.

"I'm sure."

Semele slid the books haphazardly across the floor. "Are you sure that didn't happen?"

"Yes," the girl said, laughing.

"That's right. You're right. One thing happened and not another thing."

"Yes."

"Now imagine everything. All things that are, or have ever been, happened one way and not another, no matter how chaotic or quantum or bizarre. History happened. And it happened one way. And most people don't share that story. And that's how you and I fit into the world, my little popsicle."

The little girl had no idea what her mother was talking about.

Then they went out for ice cream.

That happened to be the day Arjun left.

There had been constant fighting since Taer moved in. Always in a distant bedroom and always in convoluted language the girl couldn't fathom. She would often get involved by trying to climb onto Arjun. He would never refuse her and the conflict dispelled or was put on pause, often because it made him put his drink down.

The girl didn't know this was the last fight but felt something strange in the way Arjun walked towards the front door. When he tried to lift the girl from his shoulders, she wouldn't let go. Arjun spoke softly, trying to coax her to let go, but she dug deeper. He had to tear hair from his scalp to remove her, her strength too great.

4 – IMPATIENT PARENTS

Floating and confined in total blackness felt exquisitely primal until she realized she would soon drown. And then all manner of difficulties would begin.

Letting out precious air to orient herself, she untangled herself from the net, dragged her powerful arms through the black water and once again broke the surface of the Aegean Sea. She considered shouting at the boat, which was disappearing around the jagged southern coast of Attica, but it felt counterproductive. There was a lot to think about and some alone time seemed invaluable. Leopold was in good hands.

Her flowing robe made swimming an extra chore, so she slipped out of it, tied it around her middle, and made for shore. The water was bone chilling and the air worse when she climbed out onto a smooth rock at the base of the cliffside. The same cliffside, she was more than a little excited to note, that gave the sea its name after the legendary suicide of Medea's ex-husband and King of Athens, Aegeus. She wrung out her drenched wrap as if washing the blood of the monarch off the rocks, then had a seat.

He killed himself because he'd made a deal with his son, Theseus, who was returning from dispatching the Minotaur. His floppy-haired hero-son told his dad that he'd replace the ship's black flag with a white one so dad would know he succeeded. When Aegeus saw a black flag flying, he jumped. Hearing this story as a child, Brink found the monarch's lack of patience infuriating. It turned out, Theseus, like most boys, just neglected the chore of changing flags.

A droopy moon threw grey light on the long walls of the settlement above her. Sounion's role during the war between Athens and Sparta was to play repository for the nearby silver mines. The existence of the fortification pleased her. It was physical evidence that she and Leopold had generated the right time, but that meant the old man was, as suspected, a troubling anomaly. She got to work pouring over the data to find what had gone wrong, but eventually, sitting naked at the base of a rocky cliff, her shivering body became too distracting.

The wall was lower where the cliff added natural defense. Spartans never attacked one at a time, so she felt somewhat safe with her movements and decided to make her way up the precipice. Her hazelnut skin made her almost invisible against the winter grass and tan earth. When she reached the top, and pulled herself carefully atop the wall, Poseidon, lit by oil lamps, was there to greet her, a massive statue inside a marble temple, glowing brightly as if cut out of the black night around it. She turned to mirror his possessive look over the Mediterranean. She thought about the solemn significance to Poseidon's position, who at the far southern end of the peninsula where powerful Athens was both protected her great naval power and looked into an already ancient past, a time when he, and the life-giving power of the sea, was far more significant than the mental electric Zeus.

Brink knew the geologic history of the region, how the Mediterranean filled in five million years before and how Africa

19

would eventually crush it against Europe fifty million years from now. But she found that no matter how much time she spent preparing for the single week she planned to spend near the end of Athens' golden age, she could barely wrap her head around how much there was to know. And she was only here to get tickets for a play.

Brink's IMAC had placed her and Leopold in a perfect recreation of January, 411 BCE. By that date, all the Greek gods and goddesses were already ancient, the legends generations past. Athens was little more than a village when the island culture to the south flourished, a thousand years before the simulation date. The story of Theseus's voyage to save the children of Athens from being killed by the Minotaur at the center of the Labyrinth was about that power shift.

Worship of the bull was strong everywhere in the ancient world. In Minoan Crete, as early as 1400 BCE, there was a dangerous competition among elite children who performed ritual bull-leaping and other cow-centric tricks, a kind of highly religious olympic rodeo, long before there were cowboys and even long before there were olympics. The palace where the games took place was of elaborate design, especially to foreign competitors. The Athenian kids could certainly think of the experience as being in a maze.

That strange true history turned into the far stranger "myth" — King Minos was foolish enough to try and keep a beautiful white bull that was supposed to be sacrificed for the god of the sea. An enraged Poseidon had Daedulus create a mechanical bullsuit and put Minos's wife inside. The Queen became pregnant from the white bull, and their child, the Minotaur, was forced to live at the center of yet another Daedulus invention, the

Labyrinth, this time directed by an enraged King Minos. After a war with Athens, Minos forced the small northern settlement to send nine kids a year to be eaten by his stepson, resolved only when the Athenian king sends his son to kill the Minotaur.

While Brink distractedly thought about the mother of the bull, Pasiphaë and whether she loved her son, her musings were concluded abruptly by two heavy hands grabbing her waist and yanking her down from the wall.

Two guards wore an expression of desire and confusion.

"Cover yourself," said one, unfastening his cape and tossing it her way.

"Who do you belong to?" asked the other.

"This deliciously warm cape, sir," she said, her teeth chattering.

There was nothing metaphorical about how this evening would end if she stuck around, so, with a thank you and a polite wave goodbye, she took a few bounding steps, hopped back over the wall, and scurried off into the dark landscape.

She settled into a comfortable patch of sloped land surrounded by an abundance of dry kindling. Using strips and fibers of her robe, a strong stick, rocks, pressure, and a well-designed pit, she had a fire in a few minutes.

The night's spectral light and the blurry orange heat gave the surrounding hills the look of lazy, snoozing monsters. She felt like joining them. She draped her clothing over a bush, then got cozy.

She was a naked woman sitting alone, blinded to the world around her by her own fire. It was difficult to hide the light since there was nothing but shrub-sized foliage around, cascading hills her only real cover, but she was far from the fortification and they were unlikely to bother with her. Unfortunately, the inhabitants

21

of Sounion weren't the only souls in the area. She'd been the focus of several sets of eyes peering at her from the darkness shortly after the fire was lit.

The only thing that kept the staring men from attacking was, once again, her face. Generally, Greek men regarded women as incomplete men, laughable and good for little more than care of the home. Brink's appearance forced these men to reconsider their position on the matter. There are very few first-person accounts of humans meeting gods (zero, in fact) in Greek literature, so if a strange-looking woman was alone in the countryside at night, the thinking was most likely that she was being punished, insane, some inexplicable barbarian, a slave, or lost. Though it crossed many of their minds that she could be a god, it was quickly dismissed. These men had seen too much of the world.

They whispered among themselves about her value. It was undeniable that she was beautiful, and her body was of a popular shape at the time, especially for the current market, tall but wide-hipped with a big, round bottom. Under normal circumstances, Brink could outrun almost anyone, but her fabric had dried and she wrapped herself for maximum comfort, minimum movement. By the time Brink could hear them, their plan made audible from involuntary excitement, it was too late to correct the absurd defensive blunder she'd made. She was grabbed, hooded, and tied firmly before she had time to get free and put up a fight.

Hoping for local boys out for a quick joy ride, Brink was disappointed to once again hear the whine and creak of planks. From their language and smell, she concluded she'd been nabbed by an adversary she completely failed to consider – ancient pirates. She was kept in a cage for the night, her captors quickly learning, after broken bones and several dislodged teeth, she was not a woman to allow too much freedom.

5 – STORMY AND SOLITAIRE

The Friesian next door, jet black and moody, was never frightened when lightning struck. She wondered if that's why Mr. Tran named him Stormy. The girl wondered whether it was a problem in his brain. She could see his body react, so it wasn't deafness or any lack in his senses. His best buddy, Solitaire, a Florida Cracker, always freaked out during the nights the sky exploded in arteries of purply-white, as he should! She asked Mr. Tran, a geneticist who assisted with the area's feral horse problem, if she could have him when he died. The horse's owner, who never denied the girl anything when it came to his beloved animals, politely avoided an answer.

Before that evening's storm, the day started warm and blue. Taer and the girl spent the afternoon at Arcosanti enjoying an open-air performance of Lysistrata. Well, the girl did at least. She usually dreaded spending time alone with the bossy and inflexible Taer, and it was no different that day. Taer almost had to drag her to the auditorium seat, insisting she would definitely leave the girl to spontaneously combust in the locked car with the windows up.

Taer had been looking forward to the play for almost a year, reminding the girl of that fact several times on the drive south.

The girl found herself transfixed by the strange plot, flowing robes, and highly adult themes and costumes. She also noted Taer being transported. She'd never seen her mother's hard friend vulnerable before. The happy dumb look on her face struck her with peculiar disgust. Without thinking, she leapt out of her seat and ran down to the stage, interrupting the actors by clomping around with her arms out like an airplane, shouting with the intonation of the chorus, "This makes no sense. This makes no sense," before simulating a plane crash and after her roll, opening up her arms to the audience to sing, "But it truuuue, men do suuuuck!"

The intrusion, deemed adorable by the actors and some of the audience, who may have been familiar with the fact that an ancient Greek audience would be very loud and involved as the play went on, did not amuse Taer. She marched towards the petrified child, lifted her up, carried her back to the car, and drove home silently. The girl felt normal again.

Dark clouds came suddenly when they got home, filling the sky with dread.

The girl went to see Stormy. She carefully examined his behavior, tried to imagine the world from his point of view, walking around as if her eyes were on opposite sides of her head. The horse, who normally flirted by tossing his long, luscious mane around, ignored her. He stayed deep inside the paddock. She squeezed through the wood fence. Something was bothering Stormy. She felt like it was her fault. As if she smelled wrong.

She went home.

"If you know I know she's sick, why are you always trying to keep me away from her?" she asked Taer, whose shape perfectly blocked the doorway to Semi's bedroom.

"She needs to rest," she said, roughly tousling the seven-year-old's mass of tangled, curly hair.

"I know you want her all to yourself, but she really loves Arjun and always will," the girl said calmly, before stomping away on the wood floor hallway with the same rhythm of her earlier performance. She didn't get far before she could feel the air change and the floor rumble. Over her shoulder she saw Taer, eyes full of blood, coming at her like a rabid animal. Taer spun her around, dug her fingers into her arm, and shoved her broad finger in the girl's face. She held her words as long as she could, the pressure in her cheeks and forehead a bursting dam. And then quietly, eyes blind with tears, she said, "You. You. Disgusting. Creature. This is your fault. Your mother is dying and it is your fault." Her finger still trembling and pointing, she released the girl's shoulders, "You better be worth this. Fucking monster," her voice trailing as if she'd run out of oxygen.

There were no more sounds. Everything was clear and serene, like the end of a torrential rain.

The girl felt as if she were falling. As if the world had let go of her.

Taer turned around, hiding her tears, her guilt, walked into Semele's bedroom, and shut the door behind her.

The girl kept tumbling inside. Her knees gave out. She couldn't breathe. Her wide eyes were distant, dry.

She walked next door, a hollow saunter. Stormy wasn't outside. There was a lightning strike, but no sound. It was raining somewhere close. She walked towards the dark clouds. The next thing she knew she woke up on a bus, staring at rain flow across the window like hurtling comets. She got off and stood quietly. By the time the bus left the rain was gone and the sun was leaving red scars on the horizon.

Arjun met her at the depot. She had no memory of contacting him. He explained that she couldn't stay the night because they were coming to pick her up very soon. All she paid attention to was the hug Arjun gave her as soon as she arrived. She held that hug in her mind as she changed her wet clothes, had some soup, paced around waiting, and collapsed on the couch, resting her head on his lap.

She opened her eyes to her mother's smiling face.

Semele rubbed her forehead with a warm hand, drew her fingers through her hair carefully, fixing tangles as only she could. She kissed the girl's little nose and squeezed her tightly. She asked her daughter in a gentle tone, "Taer said she told you it was your fault I'm sick. Is that what she said?"

"Yes."

"What do you think she meant by that?"

"I don't care."

Semele sat the girl up. "I want you to tell me what she meant."

"Your cancer was caused by growing a monster inside you."

"Is that what she said?" Semele said, calmly.

"That's what she meant."

"No," Semele said. "Keep trying."

She sat up straight and answered, "You got cancer in your uterus which spread and it was probably sort of caused by me and your earlier pregnancies," the girl said evenly.

"Nope."

"That's it. That's what she meant," the girl insisted.

"Brink, you're already at an age where I can barely keep up with your mind. There is something you must learn or you're going to be lost inside there."

"I already knew it," Brink said. "As soon as I heard where the cancer started."

Semele winced. "Yes, it's true. And I should have known you'd put that together, but let's get something straight, scientist to scientist, young lady. The reason I have cancer is no one's fault. No one. But the reason I'm dying is because I'm an idiot. Entirely my fault. I ignored perfectly obvious symptoms far too long for a cancer that was pretty beatable. Now," Semele throat closed up for a moment. She tried to hide the emotion with a cough. Brink fought the instinct to cry.

"We both know Taer, as smart as she is," Semele continued, evincing an eye roll from Brink. "She's extremely intelligent, don't underestimate her. But we both know she wouldn't imagine you'd make that connection this young. You may think all she meant was to hurt you with that knowledge. But that wasn't it. I want you to tell me what it was. What did she really say?"

"I am in unbearable pain losing the person I love and to dispel some of that pain, I'm going to create a convincing scapegoat," Brink said, her voice trembling and breath straining.

"Exactly right. Had you figured that out sooner, you could have saved me a drive in the rain," Semele said, taking Brink's hands.

"You shouldn't have come," Brink said, doing her best to sound brave. "I'm going to live with Arjun now."

"No. You're not." She let out a little laugh-cry. "I love Arjun. I love him dearly. And I know you do too. But I will not make two stupid mistakes for your life."

Arjun was in earshot, but left the room to the girls. Taer was outside in the car. "The most important thing in the world is that," Semele's throat swelled again, her eyes growing wet, her vision blurring. She couldn't hold it in. She shuddered with a deep sob that tore into the core of the girl, who herself fell apart.

At this point, Arjun intervened, with tissues and water, entering the room like a soft cloud. They drew him closer and all hugged and cried. Semele got herself together, gave Arjun a deep kiss, and asked him to give her a few more minutes. He stepped away and found himself wandering outside to speak with Taer.

Brink laid against Semele, tucking under her arm. Semele easily hid her body's pain.

"First of all, I'm not going anywhere for a while, so you can just forget going anywhere but right here next to me. Taer's in big trouble. I'm not so forgiving to adults as you know. But Taer is strong. I need you protected. Safe. That's the most important thing in the world. And Arjun isn't well. You know that. He couldn't handle you. Not yet at least."

Brink filed the last phrase. It protected her from the present.

When they left, Brink gave Taer a hug. Taer looked as if she'd been eviscerated and needed one. Brink fell fast asleep on the ride home, and opened her eyes when she heard a mud-covered Stormy, kicking and rubbing against his fence, trying to get Brink's attention.

6 – TO LIGHTNING …

Leopold's eyes opened to darkness. Large drops of rain thumped around the cabin like a drunk on a broken drum. A universe-swallowing snore joined in. It was too deep, too grisly to belong to Brink.

He stood and almost tripped over another slumbering body, also not Brink.

He made his way nervously up creaking steps and was surprised to find himself on a boat. He was also surprised, and then disturbed, to find a group of men shaking and mumbling at the far end of the deck.

Brink wouldn't answer his call and he couldn't find her anywhere. He started to panic.

The dark sky burst into blinding whiteness.

Rippling showers of lightning lit the terror and guilt on the men's faces in harrowing strobe. Leopold turned towards the light-scarred night to see what gripped them. A crackling boom of thunder knocked him off his feet.

Far off, along the edge of the dark horizon, the sea began to rise. Waves tumbled skyward, a mountain range of water rising up, then smoothing into a long, organic shape, the contour of a man's back. A crouched, impossible liquid behemoth struggled to stand, weighed down by the world falling out of him, rock and coral and fish and mud. As its head began to rise, the lightning came again, golden and thick this time, almost viscous. When it struck, the world slowed. The rain in front of Leopold's face fell like snowflakes.

Arcs of dancing electric met the murky water with a deafening pop. The tentacled, xanthous sparks became two mighty arms, pushing on the shoulders of the aqueous giant. The entire sea began to boil and illuminate, a green glow swirling into a nebula of color beneath the surface. The sky grew brighter than day.

Leopold closed his eyes and waited for the world to explode.

Everything went quiet. The night was black and still.

The rain fell normally again, but soon picked up pace, a brewing storm.

Leopold searched more thoroughly for Brink, the dark hold, the sides, the crevices, as growing winds howled about the ship. He shouted, "Where is she? Have you seen a woman? Where is she?" Though he accidentally screamed in English, the crew understood his tone, the sound of a child lost and alone. They didn't ignore him. They were simply consumed by prayer. He looked back out at the sea and the horizon was once again swollen, this time by a recognizable phenomenon.

"There's a wave!" Leopold shouted. "It's coming!" He caught himself this time and pointed, "κυμαίνω!"

The men saw it, something they could understand, react to. Mortal instincts moved them about the boat, some on the sails, some on the oars, pointing the boat at the shoreline.

The coast was close but time was short.

Leopold rushed down to the cabin, where the old man and his servant still slept soundly. He kicked, then stepped over the man on the floor, and firmly but carefully shook the old man awake.

Diphon was up in an instant and grabbed Leopold's arm.

"We have to get off the boat," Leopold told him, pulling out of Diphon's grasp and helping the old man to his feet. "Come on." Diphon ran up the steps to see what could inspire such concern. The wave was almost upon them. It was cresting, creating a low, deafening rumble.

Diphon turned to help his master up the steps and began thanking him for a wonderful life. Leopold cradled the old man in his arm, and, to the servant's utter shock, rose, hovering above the deck. Leopold told the servant to grab hold of his neck, hoping to get to at least one of the sailors before the wave was on them.

Leopold launched into the air, but was only just ahead of the wall of water.

He couldn't get to any of the crew before the colossal wave sucked the ship up and crushed it as if by a squeezing fist. He quickly deposited the still sleeping old man and Diphon on high rocks along the dark beach, then raced back to the settling tumult, searching desperately for where to dive. The boat hadn't resurfaced. He could see none of the men or hear anyone shouting for help.

The sea settled. The rain was a light dancing drizzle. Leopold hung limply, inches above the green-black surface, lost in a long stare at nothing. He heard the old man's distant cough and returned to the survivors.

Diphon immediately fell to his knees in reverence. The old man looked out at the empty sea and asked, "Where is she?"

Leopold's eyes went wide. "You saw someone with me?"

"Of course."

"She wasn't... I couldn't... tell me she wasn't on the boat," said Leopold.

"When I went to sleep," the old man said, taking a breath, "she was."

"No," Leopold said tremulously.

He rocketed out to sea, slowing for a moment unsure where the wreck could be, before he split the surface. He dove deep, searching blindly through the cold blackness. He found the bottom of the sea by crashing into it. He flung himself about, colliding with rocks and tangling in plants.

Diphon pulled on the shivering old man, imploring him to move, but he used what was left of his strength to resist, saying, "We wait."

Diphon pleaded with his master, "He will find us. Gods have their ways to find us. We are close to Brauron, by blessing. Please let me get you inside."

"This is not the behavior of a god, Diphon. Open your eyes. This is a boy in the dark who has lost his only light."

Leopold came back up spinning, scanning the coast for movement. He saw nothing but settling waves disappearing in the marsh and sand. He searched everywhere. He beat the water. He screamed. He considered racing at the horizon towards the figures now quiet and asleep. But stopped himself.

He wasn't exhausted. He put his head down into his sunken shoulders, squeezed the despair out of his eyes, and rose slowly. He collected himself. He thought calmly. His panic was born more out of disconnection. He knew Brink was fine. She said this could happen. She'll be back, he assured himself.

He returned to the survivors, the aide wiping frozen tears, the old man a chalky blue. Diphon was reverent, though urgent. "I implore you. My master needs dry clothes. There is a town very near. We are acquainted with the priest. We are so close I swear I could smell the wood of his stove."

Leopold reached out to lift them again, but Diphon bowed his head and said with an apprehensive wince, "There is a temple for Artemis there," hoping she and Leopold were on friendly terms. Leopold ignored the question he didn't understand, quickly lifted them again, and hurried to the village.

As they traveled, Leopold had to be careful not to break their legs on the treetops. Preoccupied, he barely noticed the tall, sparse trees that covered the countryside. Diphon pointed out the priest's home. Leopold landed a short distance away from the fire-lit window inside the small mudbrick home, and carried the old man to the front door. Diphon pounded. A grey-haired man with a massive chest and a wide chestnut face welcomed them inside.

They stoked the hearth so the room was thick with heat, but Leopold remained numb. He leaned against a wall and stared at the floor. Diphon pitied him for his loss, and sang. The old man regained his strength quickly and went to another room with the man of the house.

Leopold felt the song reverberate through his worn body. The warmth and the sound helped him slip into a sleepy calm.

A girl came in the front door, out of breath and excited. The woman of the house scolded her for barging in, that she had no business there, and in the same breath, told her to make the visitors some barley soup. Leopold noted she had big, familiar eyes. The closer she got to him, the more he felt the warmth of the hearth at the center of the room, smelled the odors of the villager's life, heard the cry of distant wolves and nearby crickets.

It made him imagine being stuck in this world, which in turn, made him feel dizzy and sick. He had an impulse to walk out the door and keep going in one direction, forever.

The men came back out and everyone sat. Leopold had a few mouthfuls of the soup and even less of the wine. He didn't speak, but he could follow what few things were said, all of which, in some way, pertained to this mysterious girl.

After dinner, the family said a prayer in honor of the sailors and expressed tactful joy that their friend, whom they shared many meals with before, had survived. They were careful not to mention Brink. The omission meant to imply she was fine, which Leopold assumed was one of the things the old man discussed with the man of the house.

The man of the house stretched and yawned. The old man took Leopold outside.

"I do not know what you are, but from the short time I knew your companion, I know you are special to her and that you must be in great pain."

"She's fine," Leopold said, trying to end the conversation.

"I hope what you say is true," he said, taking Leopold's hand.

"She told me to meet her in Athens if something like this happened. If you're okay, and you don't mind, I'll go there now."

"This is indeed a fateful day," he went on. "The young one inside is in need of an escort. She is to be delivered to Delphi, by way of the great city. I would be deeply grateful if you could chaperone and deliver her."

"Now?"

"No. They will not allow her to travel at night. You should feel welcome making this your home. You will be given a comfortable bed."

Leopold put his hands on his head and squeezed his eyes, hoping to wake up.

"The girl's guardians are in your debt, you are free to do whatever you wish."

"I'll see you in the morning," Leopold said as he walked away.

"I will tell them."

Leopold lifted into the air, this time fully retracting his cosmetic legs, and looked around the strange little village. There was a strong smell of wood smoke on the damp night air. As fires extinguished, the homes disappeared into the dark.

7 – TWF DOI

Taer wandered around Brink's room reading an old notebook she found in a desk while hunting for double-sided tape. Her mouth was agape like a feeding whale shark. She held it preciously, making a table of her hands, her eyes straining to capture every sloppily scrawled word. The cover of the notebook had caught her attention. There was a heavy black line for the title, "A Declaration of Interdependence," and surrounding it, a dozen sketches of a logo scrawled on the tattered cover, each like a little snake with lines cutting the tail and head. The crosses created a lowercase T on the left and the higher, cresting wave of the snake's head on the right, an F, with a wavy W in between. The first page was filled with a different design with the same letters, this time like fallopian tubes, still somehow spelling T W F the T and F swirling off left and right. The next page was blank. And then, in bold pen and square letters across the middle — "the twf feminesto."

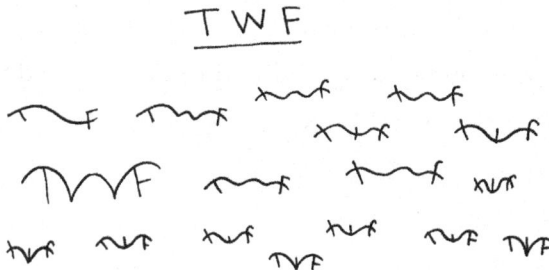

She devoured the pages, which expanded from the declaration to a list of masculine missteps through history and into a life-affirming plan for how to grow healthy cities, ending with a call to arms for the women of the world for solidarity and action. Taer wasn't sure whether she was on her third or fourth read when Brink walked in.

"How did you write this?" Taer asked breathlessly.

Brink, who was supposed to be at a sleepover, marched towards Taer and tore the notebook from her hands.

"Careful!" Taer shouted like a panicked archivist.

"Why are you in my room?" Brink shouted back, fangs showing.

"We must talk about this."

"Get out," Brink said with a dangerous look in her eye.

Taer feared the girl's physical strength, but felt invincible after what she'd read.

"What does the T W F stand for?" asked Taer.

Brink, having reacted instinctively to her bull-headed guardian, finally heard her tone, saw her suppliant posture. It threw her off. She fought the idea that what calmed her was some authentic human connection, that the impossible-to-please parent had finally recognized the value of the child.

"Just leave," Brink said.

"Darling, you need to listen to me," Taer said quietly, making her deep voice a soothing massage. "I've been a terrible parent for you. I've done nothing to encourage your skills, mostly from never being around because I didn't think you needed me, but also because I've done nothing to earn your respect."

It wasn't what Brink expected to hear. It wasn't something Brink thought Taer was capable of saying. It was as if she was turning her own manipulative power on herself in one last attempt to win Brink over. It was sort of working.

Taer continued, "I don't know where this came from, I mean I know it's exactly you, your voice, your amazing mind, but I want you to know I can feel it against me like a hurricane, a cleansing, beautiful wind, and I get it and I want it. I want it for everyone."

"It's not a hurricane," Brink interrupted, thrilled, though hiding it, by Taer's enthusiasm. "It's a wave. The final wave. TWF stands for Tidal Wave Feminism. But I wrote it in a huff when I was a kid. It's mostly nonsense I think."

Tears filled the eyes of the adult who for the first time, felt bonded to the child she was responsible for. "May I hold on to it?"

"I don't care," Brink said, tossing the document on her bed. "Just stay out of my room."

Brink grabbed her jacket and left with a tight smile.

The next day all was normal again. Taer wasn't home. The elation from the hope she'd be there to talk about the ideas in the notebook evaporated. Brink barely took note of it missing from her bed.

A week went by and Brink hadn't heard from Taer. It wasn't unusual for Taer to disappear on business trips, or whatever they were. But for the first few days, she couldn't let go of the hope that a new relationship had begun. Eventually she got back into the swing of things and went over to Porter's.

Porter expected her daily and could usually predict her arrival time. He was surprised to see her early that day.

He'd converted an old turkey shed into a long comfortable house filled with books and surrounded by rare rose species. A retired academic from California, he moved to the area many years ago and built a successful solar farm. He was one of the early residents to encourage and cultivate the growing population of research scientists. He had energy to spare and was feeling lonely in his old age so he cherished his visits from the town's favorite daughter. Brink had clear memories of many drunken bridge games at the house with her mom, Arjun, Sandi, and Porter, whom she thought of like an uncle.

Brink had her lab next to Porter's house where she roped him and many other residents into her research. Over the years since her mother passed, Brink had far surpassed her mother's work, and inadvertently developed patents as she customized technology and medication related to her investigations. Arjun found a colleague to help her with the filings and she put him in charge of her royalties, which grew immense by the time she was twelve.

"I think I hate her in a totally new way," Brink said, tucking herself in Porter's favorite reading chair.

"Sounds like a breakthrough," Porter said, appearing with a plate of sweetly seasoned charcuterie. He kissed her head and held the plate at a distance so she'd follow it, get up, and get out of his chair. She rubbed his belly as she took the plate, and went to her favorite window seat.

"I'm like your really expensive cat," she said, soaking in the sun and getting drowsy.

He ignored her. He could tell she was more preoccupied than usual and wouldn't stay long.

"I don't have time for this today," she announced, pretending he was insistent she stay.

"I'm out of here, man," she cried, standing up.

40

"Cats are so predictable."

Rubbing her forehead along Porter's, she made a goodbye purr sound before skittering out the door.

The sun was a bright yellow ball against an empty blue sky, the air a brisk giddy bite on the flesh, which put Brink in an especially good mood when she got home. It made the sight of a man's leather biker jacket draped on the dining room table with an embroidered TWF emblem on the back dizzyingly surreal. She worried she might be in a dream for a moment. The letters, in the form somewhat like her own swirly version, were corded gold against a midnight blue background. It took her another examination to notice the bold and capital CALIFORNIA in a smiley curve beneath the patch. Of course gold. Perfect color for when she peed on it, she thought. She lifted it off the chair with two fingers as if it were a filthy rag and headed for the bathroom when Taer came in the front door, jogging headphones in, her husky arms and sturdy legs seizing when she saw Brink.

Taer muttered an expletive under her breath before employing a gift-giving tone, "Do you like it?"

"Oh I love it," Brink replied, mocking her business mode, "I love how you stole my little girl ramblings and especially love how it implies you're moving to California. When do you leave?"

Before she could reply, the owner of the jacket, a stout man, out of breath and also in form-fitting running clothes, came inside behind Taer. It was not uncommon for Taer to bring home playmates, but when Brink put the scene together and imagined the convolutions required to put the logo, jacket, man, and woman together, she felt the coolness of the day return, as if she'd been let out of a locked box she'd been trapped in since her mom died. She let the jacket drop to the ground, walked to her room,

41

threw a few things in a bag, came back out to the kitchen, put a pear and two handfuls of nuts in her bag, and said, as she strolled past the sweaty couple, "Make sure the checks are made out to my business. If you need me, I'll be living with my lawyer."

— in the earnest handwriting of a young half-bonobo:

IN MY BEDROOM, nevermore July 4th, 1776

The unequivocal Declaration of a seven year old girl in the united States of America,

When the Course of human events unnecessarily dissolve the ecological bonds which have connected people and Nature, and taking for granted the powers of the earth by investing them in a singular anthropomorphic Creator who entitles them to Nature, a decent respect to the opinions of all humans require they should declare the causes which impel them to reunite.

We hold these truths to be self-evident, that most males are created short-sighted and violent, that they are endowed by their Parents with certain unearned Privileges, that among these are Superiority, Ownership, and the pursuit of Power. --That to secure these privileges, Governments have been instituted among Men, deriving their overwhelming power from the manipulation of the governed, --That whenever any Form of Community becomes destructive of these ends, it is the obligation of considerate people to encourage it, and to institute new government, laying its foundation on holistic principles and organizing its powers in such form, as to them shall seem most likely to effect their Balance with Earth. Prudence, indeed, will dictate that governments long established should not be changed for light and transient causes; and accordingly all experience has shown, that women are more disposed to suffer, while evils are sufferable, than to right themselves by abolishing the forms to which they are accustomed. But when a long train of abuses and usurpations, pursuing invariably the same Object evinces a design to reduce them under absolute Patriarchy, it is their responsibility, their necessity, to throw off such Governments, and to provide new Guards for their future security.-- such has been the patient sufferance of Women and Kind Men; and such now is the necessity which constrains them to alter their former Systems of Government. The history of Masculine rule is a history of repeated injuries and usurpations, all having in direct object the establishment of an absolute Tyranny over the resources and spirit of our planet. To prove this, let facts be submitted to a candid world.

8 – ... AND TIGERS

Leopold woke to the roar of bears, four little she-bears, dressed in yellow gowns and crowns of sticks and fur shaped into soft, round ears. They howled to announce themselves. They howled to frighten and hold their ground. They howled to show their visitor love. He tensed up and buried his face in his heavy blanket. The girls laughed and pulled his covering away, revealing his lithe brown body, quite nude, which surprised Leopold more than his growling alarm clocks. He had no memory of disrobing. He quickly rolled onto his stomach and let himself yell out, "Hey!" hoping that would suffice as a "Get out!" It didn't, but the girls were soon shooed away by Iphitheme, the woman of the house. They did their best throaty, disappointed moans with trailing titters.

Iphitheme placed a tray of olives and bread on a low wood table. Averting her eyes, she took the freshly washed chiton that was draped over her arm and placed it on the side of the bed saying, "Anything you require I will provide." Her voice was as soothing as a bath. Leopold thanked her awkwardly. As she made her way out, he was struck by the swinging heft of her shape, the light from the open doorway framing her voluptuous body.

After dressing, Leopold marched outside without a word. He didn't notice the shocked faces of his hosts.

When he sensed he was out of view, he lifted himself up into the sky and moved towards a solitary promontory. He disrobed and stretched his arms towards the sun, soaking in the energy hungrily.

Returning to the house, with a wide, well-lit view below him, he was surprised to notice the village was larger than he expected with lines of little chalky-colored homes and small farms, stone bridges over creeks, and a dramatic walkway to a bank-like building which he thought must be the temple Diphon mentioned for Artemis.

There was a large group of people he either hadn't noticed before or arrived while he was away. He landed out of sight and ran over, worried they were waiting on him.

The girls in the bear costumes were dancing about at the front of the gathering. Leopold saw the girl in the middle of them. Her hair was pulled back with wide braids and an interlocking, serpentine garland. Her eyes were emerald green and she squinted and smiled when she saw him, squirming her way out of the crowd to greet him.

When the rest of them saw Leopold approach, they looked relieved, some of the men letting out audible lamentations, the sound of strings and woodwinds rang out, and the villagers became a hurly-burly moving forward.

The old man, indebted and concerned, broke away and with a broad smile, took Leopold's hand, drawing him towards the procession.

The girl ran to them, pulled Leopold down to face her, kissed his head and graced it with a laurel wreath. She leapt away gleefully and rejoined the head of the revelers.

At the same moment, a Brian Eno flourish invaded Leopold's thoughts. He shouted, "Holy shit!"

Seeing the shocked look on the old man's face, he continued, "It's Brink!" This didn't help the old man understand, but he was happy to see not only Leopold moving along with the festive march, but his face alive with joy and reassurance.

"You okay?" Brink asked.

"What happened?!"

"I managed to get myself kidnapped."

"You what!? Where are you? I'll come get you."

"No. No. I'm fine, but it's going to take a little time to get back to Athens. I'm not able to get a look at your situation but your vitals are weirdly mellow. What are you up to?"

"I'm in a parade. Maybe a birthday party? I'm not sure what's going on. I've been asked to walk a girl to Athens."

Brink laughed, which immediately became a grunt.

"You okay?" asked Leopold.

"Yeah, good good. It's a strain to work this side of my body," Brink sighed. "What happened to the boat?"

"There was a storm that made no sense and the boat was wrecked and there were a couple dudes who I took to a nearby town."

"Oh no, was there an older guy?"

"Yeah, he's the one who asked me to help the girl."

What the hell is going on, thought Brink.

"I'm walking next to him right now, actually."

"Say hi from me!"

There was a long pause.

"Wait, you're not actually saying hi from me, are you?"

"He gave me a 'you poor thing' face."

Brink laughed again, "Ow ow ow."

"Are you okay to keep doing this?"

"Of course. Aren't you having a good time?"

"I'm fine, but like, aren't you in trouble?"

"It's exciting! But yeah, I should get back. You okay for a bit? It's going to take a lot of catch-up to get to a place I can chat again. Have you pulled up any maps?"

"You told me not to!"

"Do whatever you need to to stay safe."

"Oh, there's a highly rated fish place not too far from here. I mean you know thousands of years from now. We should check that out."

"I gotta run. You good?"

"Sure, yeah. I think I'm just spending the day walking."

"Lucky you, it's beautiful out," Brink said as she remembered the sun kissing her body on the pirate ship as her real body was going numb from straining. "Talk to you as soon as I can."

"Okay, I guess."

Leopold felt the disconnect somewhere in his bioplastic guts.

Leopold was growing anxious. He saw the walk to Athens was at least seven hours and the morning was draining away.

Finally, after a tearful farewell from what felt like the whole settlement, it was time to depart. Packed bags were handed to the girl. Leopold tried to take a heavy satchel, but she yanked it from him and strapped it to her back. He didn't argue, gathered the rest, and followed her on a path over the low hills to the north.

The girl was peeling away from Leopold, heading west. He asked why she was going that way.

The girl didn't answer, but another voice did from some distance behind them, "It is the safest way to go. We follow the coast."

Leopold spun around. She snorted at his defensive stance.

The voice belonged to a boy who sidled up to the girl. Leopold jogged in front of them and stopped, waving his arms like a truant officer.

"Hey. Hey. Wait a minute. Who is this?"

"This is my Amyntas," she answered.

"I will not let her travel without me, especially since this is the last time I will see her," said her Amyntas.

"This is your secret boyfriend?"

They walked past him.

"Hold on," Leopold commanded, surprising himself with the convincing tone.

They waited and listened. "I'm going this way," he said, pointing towards the mountains in the north. "That means you are too."

"It is not safe that way. I've already told you that."

To the north was a mostly flat, boring plain that stretched almost all the way to the mountains. It looked about as threatening as the San Fernando Valley. He knew the mountain incline would be a bit more effort, but the route would cut their trip almost in half and he would happily carry all the bags.

The girl was excited by the idea. She had never been up Hymettus and immediately started walking in that direction. The boy took furious strides towards the girl and grabbed her. She wriggled free from his grasp and darted ahead. Leopold raced in front of her, several strides before Amyntas caught her again, his pace shocking them both.

"Let's calm down. We'll be fine this way. What is so dangerous up there?"

"He's scared to be caught with me," said the girl.

"Caught? We're climbing over a mountain on a random path. Who could possibly know where either of you are?"

Amyntas kept angrily silent.

"That's why you're here, right? Protection," said Leopold. "You protect her and I'll protect both of you."

Amyntas snarled at him, then marched out in front of the girl and walked toward the mountain as if it were his idea.

As they passed by an abandoned, scorched farm, the blackened land speckled with yellow grass and cold exposed stone that were once walls, Leopold found himself thinking about how he would survive if he were somehow trapped here.

He spent hours in a mental maze of fabrication, listing materials he needed to make an electrical generator, synthetic polymers, a supercomputer, nanorobots, the vast inventory of his special mortality. And then he thought about how he would acquire the raw materials he needed to even begin manufacturing. The reality of economics, his lack of history, and the narrow limits of his own social powers got him down.

Amyntas and the girl stopped. Leopold looked up for the first time in a while. They had arrived at the foothills of Mount Hymettus. Eager to reach his destination, and assuming they stopped because the girl finally grew weary carrying the bag, he went to take it from her. She pulled away.

Amyntas yelled, "Stop touching her. Do you not understand who this girl is?"

"Am I supposed to know?" Leopold said in English.

The indecipherable sounds inspired Amyntas to explain as if to a child, "She is to be Pythia!"

Leopold tried to hide his ignorance.

"She is chosen as vessel for shining Apollo at his most sacred temple," Amyntas said, with less piety than rage.

Amyntas threw his bag down. He took the girl's bag, sat down with her, pulled out some dense bread and a hunk of the goat they'd sacrificed earlier, covering them in a sweet-smelling oil, gave her a small amount and began gnawing away. She ate ravenously, making loud smacking sounds with her mouth.

Something about the deliberate drama of the situation struck Leopold oddly, and he asked, "Are you two actors?"

They went on eating.

"Does that word make sense to you?" he asked.

The girl laughed.

"Do you know the word sheep-anus?" asked Amyntas.

"This just seems weirdly unrealistic, which I know, doesn't even makes sense," Leopold said mostly to himself.

Swallowing, then standing and stretching, Amyntas addressed Leopold, "You talk like a woman." He strapped his bag back across his chest, picked the girl up by the arm, and they continued on their way.

The sun was getting low and purple shadows spread across the foothills like creeping pachyderms. Amyntas headed left and it took a few hundred steps for Leopold to notice he was skirting the mountain, trying to turn them west. Leopold turned right, ascending. The girl pulled away from Amyntas and hurried after

Leopold. She handed him her bag. Amyntas paused, grinding his teeth for a moment, then trudged after them.

It was slow going to the top of the range and as they neared the peak, dark green trees obscured their view and Leopold had to rely on his map.

Amyntas's grunting and discomfort grew louder. Leopold asked the girl, "Would you tell me what I'm missing here? Does your family hate his family? Why wouldn't they let him take you to wherever we're dropping you off?"

"She has no family," Amyntas interjected.

Leopold stopped. He turned and said angrily, "Look, I have no idea who you are. You're doing a spectacular job of acting like the tough guy and angry lover, but if you continue being a rude jerk, I'm gonna put you on top of that tree."

The air around them grew humid as Leopold spoke.

"I don't fear you, stranger," the boy said with his chest out.

"Well, you know what? You really should."

The bushes and trees began thickening, a forest forming outside their periphery.

The girl got between them. "No one in the village is my family. I was left there a long time ago," she said.

"This girl is descended from Phye," Amyntas growled.

Leopold's face was blank.

"The faker. Like you say. An actor. The actor who posed as Athena herself. Phye! Her line was never allowed back inside Athens. This little one, useless as a courtesan, was sent to the priests of Brauron to serve the temple. She has a clever tongue, like a man. So clever that your educated old friend insisted she be trained in rhetoric." Amyntas was almost shouting. "All that did was prepare her for the priests of Delphi."

51

Leopold finally saw the love in the boy's eyes. He backed off.

Impossibly, the foliage was growing, building a gnarled canopy, blocking out the sun.

"What is going on?" Leopold asked, finally aware of the altered scenery.

Within steps, they were in a thick knot of vegetation, a wet forest, the sounds of shrieking animals and deafening bugs filling their ears. The boy and girl drew close to Leopold for protection.

"This is why we should not have gone this way," Amyntas said.

"Why, what is this?" Leopold said, a little panicked.

A woman's voice, soft as a whisper, called out, "My brother will not show you patience as I do, little one."

Amyntas dropped to his knees. Leopold turned around like a dog looking for a teasing owner. The girl crossed her arms defiantly.

A woman emerged from the trees as if separating from them, moss and branches falling from her shoulders and hips. What little she wore was made of woven stalks and leaves. With some focus, Leopold noticed she looked very much like the girl as an adult.

"Amyntas. Stand up. You embarrass yourself."

"Is that your mother?" asked Leopold.

"Pffft," the girl replied.

Amyntas stood, surreptitiously pulling a dagger from his bag. The woman smiled and began walking back and forth like a cat. With every step, almost imperceptibly, her appearance changed.

"You would risk your life for this wisp, strong Amyntas? I'm not sure I can afford to lose one of my best at Brauron." Her voice became huskier with every word.

Short, orange fur, drizzled with streaks of tan and black, flowed out across her skin, her face grew a long white beard. She fell over and landed on clenched paws.

Leopold laughed, cathartically. "This," he stuttered, stepping forward. "I mean this feels so real. This is incredible. Ridiculous. This makes no sense at all. What the holy crap *is* this?"

"If you can hear me, something is super messed up here," he thought to Brink.

The animal growled, spit flying from its snout. Leopold tried to approach the tiger, but couldn't. It was too convincing, too horrifying.

Amyntas pulled the girl behind him and backed up carefully, but she pulled away and blasted into the woods, purposely squealing like a pig as she went, trying to attack the beast.

The tiger shifted towards her, head down, neck muscles throbbing. Amyntas lunged, yelling in as deep a tone he could. The creature was upon him, pinning him down with her massive forearms, her nose pushing against his. Leopold sprung at her, instinctively, and then recoiled just as instinctively when she roared at him, ears back, teeth dripping angry drool. She leapt off Amyntas, producing audible cracks from both his shins, shifted around, flexed her hind leg muscles, and attempted a leap to chase down the girl, but fell flat on her chin.

Leopold had grabbed her tail.

She scrambled upright, ripped her tail from his hand, and spun to face him. It looked to Leopold like she was smiling. Then she bounded off into the thick green in the opposite direction the girl had darted. Leopold ran over to Amyntas.

The boy writhed in pain, straining to keep from blacking out. His skin wasn't torn, but both his legs were bent where they shouldn't be, clearly fractured.

"Don't move," Leopold cried. He rushed around, searching the ground, and returned with two long, solid sticks. He gently pushed the bones as straight as he could, the pain in Amyntas's face bringing Leopold's immersion fully back. He splinted the sticks to each leg with Amyntas's rope belt and a torn strip of his himation, being careful not to tie them too tightly.

Amyntas made a sustained grunt to summon the energy, then uttered, "Leave me and find her."

Before Leopold could make a move, he was being shoved aside. The girl had returned, sliding on her knees to attend to Amyntas.

"What's happened to you?"

He took her hand and squeezed.

"Did she hurt you?" she asked sweetly, then stood up and raged at Leopold, hitting his chest, "You were supposed to protect us."

"I think I...," he said weakly.

He scanned the woods and said, "It will be okay. I have an idea."

He found two saplings, dry from the winter, and snapped them into pieces as long as Amyntas's legs. He returned and added the longer pieces to the current splints, wrapping them with another torn piece of wool.

Leopold lifted Amyntas carefully into his arms. The pain of being moved was horrible and Amyntas became drowsy to the point of losing consciousness. "I don't know if you should fall asleep, so stay awake," he told him.

The girl was happy to continue, grateful and impressed by Leopold's display of strength. She walked alongside, patting Amyntas's sweaty head and moving his long curls when they blew into his face.

She sang sweetly.

Leopold ignored the sound at first, distracted by the strange wrinkle to the adventure he was on. Before he could get too lost in stress, he began to notice the girl's lyrics, unusually familiar. She was telling a story of a lost child. The more attuned he became, the more the girl's voice expanded and changed. She was singing in polyphonic overtones. The vibrations echoed inside his unusual body and he felt like he was coming apart. In a good way. He felt like she were communicating to the unique creature he was, as if she somehow knew he was composed differently and figured out a frequency only he could hear.

They were soon out of the strange woods onto the normal terrain of yellow grass and thin trees.

It took them the rest of the afternoon to reach the top, Amyntas slipping in and out of a light, drowsy sleep, occasionally joining in deliriously with "regular" singing. They crested the shaded side of the mountain just after sunset. Athens stretched out below them, lamp flames painting it with a fiery golden glow.

The girl let how a howl, frightening Leopold.

It was dark by the time they reached the outskirts of the city, making their way past untended farms and endless rows of tall, thin cypress trees. They crossed a small river, which showed on Leopold's map as a "phenomenon of interest" as marked by

55

Brink. The river had been covered up and rediscovered during the construction of the first Athens Metro.

Oil lamps lit the Itonian Gate with a flicker of foreboding. The scale of everything intimidated Leopold, but it looked absurdly fake at the same time. It felt like when he first entered Disneyland and didn't know it wasn't real. He was surprised there were no guards or checkpoints of any kind as they made their way inside. The war he was told to read about between Athens and Sparta held to a general truce during winters.

Leopold's stuttering gait while gapping at the sights woke Amyntas, which was fortunate, because he was the only one of the three who had visited the city and was needed for navigation. Amyntas' sweaty scent was overpowering the strange fragrance of spice on the air. They wound through narrow streets past boxy homes with narrow windows. The fabric colors of the passersby were like none Leopold had seen, rusty, bloody reds, shiny white gold, purples like Brink's hair. And even though growing up in Los Angeles, he'd never seen so much flesh at night.

The homes became slightly larger as they rounded north of the Acropolis. Leopold was puzzled by his calm. He felt weirdly comfortable, as if absorbing the mellow style of the residents around him, the smells and sounds, the air and the colors, the music spilling out from around every corner, and passionate (or at least loud) conversation spilling out of windows.

They arrived at the house of Pyralimpes after Amyntas carefully interpreted the address from a pottery shard in one of their bags. It looked as plain, though larger, than any of the other homes they'd passed, except for the wooden door, which was ornately decorated with an elaborate owl design and the roof tiles seemed cleaner. The girl retrieved a note for the man of the house from her original bag and handed it to a servant who met them out front. Two more came to help with Amyntas. They carefully lifted him from Leopold's arms and took him around the back of the house. A red-haired and pale-skinned woman approached and took the girl's hand, escorting her inside a back room. Leopold stood in an open-air courtyard at the center of the home, alone and confused for several minutes, until an older gentleman, tall and bald with a kind, sunken face, approached him. Two young men stared down on them from a second-story terrace.

"I have read the note from our friend. You are quite welcome here," Pyralimpes said with a knowing look, hoping to communicate that Leopold's collusion with the ostracized old man was fine with him.

Leopold didn't know what the look meant, but he replied, "Thank you." He waited, hoping to hear more, but the man was quiet. "You have a lovely home," he said, trying to sound convincing as the man circled him.

"I did not expect you to be so young. You must be a favorite pupil of his. The note said you were born an Athenian but raised on Andros. That explains your queer Thracian accent."

Leopold nodded, desperate to avoid responding to any questions.

"You are quite beautiful," he said, caressing Leopold's cheek. "Your skin has the strangest luster. How I wish I could be your age again." He walked towards a couch. "You must be hungry. I will bring food and wine and you can meet my daughter. Oh, wait, she is caring for a friend. Tomorrow then. You will stay with my boys. They are eager to discuss what you've learned from your master. His expulsion from the city was absurd and was not

57

supported by this or any household in Skambonidai." Leopold kept nodding.

He asked about the boy and girl. Pyralimpes explained that the boy was resting and in good care and the girl would be ready to travel with him at first light.

"Travel with me?" said Leopold.

"To Delphi. You escort her. Is this not true?"

Damn it, thought Leopold.

"Yes. That is true," Leopold seemed obliged to answer. "I was just surprised she would be ready so soon. Maybe she wanted to have a look around the city tomorrow."

The man laughed and slapped Leopold's back. Then grabbed his shoulders, impressed with Leopold's solid, powerful torso. Leopold smiled uncomfortably.

The evening crawled as the sons, who joined when the food was served, talked about language and truth and all sorts of topics Leopold spent little time with, let alone discussed during a meal.

After a surprisingly delicious repast of quail eggs, dripping figs, and a buttery cheese, Leopold was invited to join the boys upstairs for the night.

When they got upstairs, the younger of the boys, no more than sixteen, as if waiting all evening, accosted Leopold.

"A stranger's ears are just what I need. I want to call it Athena's Lovers, though everyone advises me against it," the young man said. "I've been given a chance to show at the Lenaia as a last-minute addition, but I haven't submitted the title. There is already a comic with my name, so I'm thinking of changing it. There are only a few days until the festival, but my piece is very simple. One mask. Do you think that will bore the audience?"

"Are you performing now?" asked Leopold.

"No, no, I was just filling you in, but you are right. All meaningless," he cried as he paced about. "I shall begin."

The boy's brother left the room, shaking his head.

Leopold listened politely, smiling when he thought he should. It seemed like a comedy, but he couldn't be sure. The young man grew more and more confident, which helped. It went on for some time, the speaking parts changing, indicated by him holding up a different hand gesture to his forehead for each character. To Leopold's surprise, the play began to take form and even though names or places were a mystery, the humor was clear. He laughed at the strange loud divergent voices, he laughed at the sometimes bawdy lines, and the title of the play started to resonate, inspiring a knowing chuckle. Various members of the city tried to seduce the patron goddess, Athena, who Leopold learned at the beginning of the play was a virgin and a badass. It was naughty and profound. Leopold got it. He found himself bent forward, rapt, and when the author stopped, he clapped.

The young man smiled and bounded over to where Leopold was sitting on the bed. He lay down next to him, staring at the ceiling and started in on what needed fixing. The brother returned, went to his own bed, the only other one in the room, snuffed out the light, and went to sleep.

Leopold listened silently until the boy fell asleep mid-sentence. He considered lying on the floor, but couldn't tell if that would be rude in some consequential way, so he leaned back, and wondered if this was what having siblings was like.

9 – PAGE

Bidziil was infuriated when tourists looked at Brink with that head cock. He was happy Brink was camouflaged so she felt safe but she didn't look anything like his people. Brink, who was never comfortable with needing to hide out in the open, was inclined to pull their heads from their shoulders, but then she'd be spending all her summers drenched in blood. There was far more important work to do among the disappearing waters of Lake Powell.

Arjun insisted Brink needed socialization and should attend a public school. Brink, whose arrival inspired Arjun to get sober, could not resist his desire and agreed, though she only went for a few days, just long enough to make some great new friends her age as well as make arrangements with the principal. Brink would trade supplies and hire support staff for not mentioning her truancy to her pop.

Brink meant to spend all her time advancing her magic brain machine, but she couldn't keep her mind off the geology of the region. Something about the conflicts between man and nature and man and water and man regulating man was too compelling for her to ignore. She decided to pick up a quick PhD in Geology.

She volunteered with local paleontologists and geologists to get a firm grasp on the elemental, biological, and mineral makeup of her local universe, the slow shifting, sifting beauty of the high desert, the cool red sand beneath her bare feet that felt like home.

She tried to drag Bidziil and the gang out to bone digs regularly but they were actual schoolchildren with actual schoolchildren concerns. This didn't stop Brink from arranging field trips which turned into Earth-worshipping craft fairs more than educational trips.

The contacts and shenanigans in the area led inevitably to Brink being involved in local politics, which inspired her activism around management of the Colorado River. It gave her a reason to get back to work on her machine. With it, she'd make irresistible immersive presentations to city councils, mayors and federal representatives, illustrating how much worse things would get if water management wasn't taken seriously beyond immediate impulses, power grabs, graft, and worst of all sins, bad design.

She'd helped Page grow and get along as best she could without going full George Bailey. She'd advanced her machine to a point that required more knowledge and collaboration.

There was a lot of world. And she was almost fifteen. There was only one thing left on her to-do list.

"I need you to pick me up," Brink said into her phone to Arjun.

"I'm not driving into Escalante. Wait, are you okay?"

"Yeah, I'm fine, but I'm stuck. And I'm not out there. I'm at Mighty Kongs."

"What? Then just walk home. I'm not going out."

"I wouldn't ask if I didn't need a ride, man. Come on."

"Order me the mushroom thing."

"Sure thing. Hurry up."

Brink didn't answer the phone when Arjun arrived. Fortunately, she knew he never left the house without putting on something presentable, so when he angrily walked up to the entrance and saw someone familiar who wasn't Brink, he didn't embarrass himself.

"She told me she was stuck in the bathroom and needed feminine help," said Saoirse, a paleobiologist Brink had worked with over the few years she'd been in Page, and who had been over to the house many times. Brink noticed the incandescence between Arjun and her and neither did anything about it which had annoyed her to no end.

"I won't be home tonight! You're welcome!" shouted Brink as she rode by on her flame-colored Kawasaki, Bidziil tucked behind her laughing and pointing.

10 – ON THE ROAD TO KNOW

It wasn't that Leopold was the least bit homophobic, in fact, he happily considered himself queer, not gay or bisexual, but different from most he talked to. I mean his mother was a GD bonobo. He wasn't that concerned with gender in general, he was simply inexperienced, had someone he was fond of, and didn't want to offend when the teenage comedian snuggled him. Leopold pulled away.

"Will you join me at Simon's today?"

"I really have to go."

"Surely you can spare a few hours while we care for the girl."

"The girl?"

"The one you are delivering to the priests at Delphi."

"Right!" He said, standing up quickly.

At the opposite end of the room, from another small bed, a voice roared, "Will you two keep quiet? It is too early to rise. Are we farmers now?"

"Ignore him. That's my little half-brother, Antiphon. He thinks he is the boss of everyone because he is smarter than the rest of us."

"I'm no smarter than the dumbest citizen whom I depend on to be wise, shit-eater."

"Or we could wrestle," the young man said, trying to appeal to Leopold. "I'm very good. I've won awards."

Leopold hustled downstairs.

The teen turned to his brother, beaming. "He loved my play!"

"You're an idiot. Go back to sleep."

Leopold entered the courtyard of the house and found Pyralimpes reading. He quietly made for the front door, but had to slap his hand over his mouth to keep from shouting when Brian Eno chimed. Desperate to find a place to hide, he rolled under a low table.

"Fussmuckits, where are you?"

"Are you okay? Why are you whispering like you're spying on someone," asked a gleeful Brink.

"I'm hiding. This is a very intense household."

"I see you've made it to Athens. I am soooo jealous. Is it amazing?"

"Are you not here?"

"I am about to leave the lovely and breathtaking Corinth. I got bought by a very cute dude."

"What is wrong with you? We need to get out of here."

"No way! You don't find this fascinating?"

"It's too fascinating. You made it very clear not to treat this like a game. Well it's super-bugged. I saw a mutfungin' tiger yesterday, a *talking* tiger, in a freaking enchanted forest."

"I cannot wait to see that. Amazing. Yes, I'm still trying to figure out why things went sideways, but it looks like an easy fix. Are you in danger?"

"I'm whispering because they're expecting me to walk that girl another hundred fifty kilometers north."

"Oh good yes that really helps."

"I said a hundred and ..."

"We're being led somewhere and I have no idea why."

Leopold closed his eyes and rested his head on the floor.

"Oh shit, I've gotta go," Brink herself whispered. "We're on the move."

Leopold was quiet.

"We'll figure this out together, okay?"

"Okay. When?"

Brink was gone again.

The house's servants were preparing the courtyard altar for a morning prayer.

They pretended not to notice Leopold crawl out and stand up. He didn't see the man of the house, but noted the door open so he scurried out.

Everyone was gathered around, the send-off underway. The girl ran up to hug Leopold. She wore fresh clothes with a heavy hooded cape. Was it yellow? The colors were really messing with Leopold.

11 – PITTSBURGH F*CKS

Sherman Schulman, having been warned by the colleagues she'd already visited, and indirectly by Brink herself, was surprised how uncomfortable he was. At sixteen, with long, mostly hairless thighs, strong curvy hips, and bundles of roiling purple curls (even her face became less brow-centric), she arrived at Dr. Schulman's office in tight tiny shorts, a loose tank top, and little else. Sherman was single, late thirties, and part of the faculty at Carnegie Mellon's Human-Computer Interaction Institute. She'd saved her mother's alma mater, best for last.

He welcomed her into his cramped office, scanning the walls for an idea of what he'd left on display to incriminate him and to keep him from fixing his gaze. It wasn't that the girl was starkly attractive that made him uncomfortable. When Brink confirmed her existence to the academic world, the talk of her was sensational, disbelieving. They read the paper of her origins with frothing skepticism. That she was the inventor of the IMAC, SupRTALENs, ARRO, and held dozens of patents under a nom de plume, and that she wouldn't reveal the identities of her parents or the details of the techniques involved in her birth made it feel like he walked into a Gothic novel. Then they met her. She allowed limited brain scans, blood work, all sorts of tests, anything they liked as long as they'd discuss their own work with her. An education paid for by viscera and intellectual titillation. Within a month, there was a waiting list to meet the young woman. A list that became scandalous as she made her way around the world, though her reputation far outstripped her experience. Way too many well-behaved men and women in the world, she regretted.

"I'm honored to have you here, Ms. ... Brink? Is Brink the whole name?"

"Just Brink is good," she said. "I know how pretentious that sounds, but I haven't decided on a last name yet. I forgot to come up with a secret identity when I hit the road."

"It's not much of a secret anymore is it?" Sherman said, forgetting how tactless he was. "I didn't mean to imply you're pretentious. Or that everyone knows your secret. Oh wow. Could you go outside and come back in?"

Brink obeyed, coyly. She spun around in the doorway. "I want my mom to rest in peace, you know?"

"Of course."

"If I use her name, I feel like she's going to enter the popular imagination as Dr. Moreau."

"That makes perfect sense to me. I'm sorry if I offended you. If it's any consolation, your mother was worshipped by everyone who knew her here. I wish I'd had the pleasure of meeting her."

"She was pretty cool," Brink said, swallowing. "And there's nothing to apologize for."

Brink sat back down. "I hear you're pretty cool too, Mr. Schulman."

"That can't be true. I terrorize everyone I meet."

"Yeah, I love that. How about that tour," she said, catching him staring at her breasts. "Unless you want to make out?"

"I ..." he considered matching her playfulness and teasing, but hung there, not worried about the moral clarity but caught in a thought he couldn't quite get to. Brink had seen the face before, and helped him.

"You're wondering whether me being more or less another species makes the obviously inappropriate nature of my flirting less or more inappropriate?"

"That is exactly what I didn't realize I was trying to think," he said as if taking a breath. "I feel like I owe you an apology?"

"Because you won't make out with me?"

Schulman opened his mouth again, but could only laugh.

After two years on the road devouring knowledge, making friends and important business and political contacts, Brink found a home in Pittsburgh.

Brink sent a loving postcard to Arjun at least once a week the entire time she traveled. He collected and tacked them all onto a wall until it looked like he was solving an international murder mystery after which he put them in a nice box Saoirse bought for them.

Brink reported she'd be staying on with the research fellows at HCII and Shermy, as Brink took to calling him, became her advisor when she decided to get more degrees. Arjun was thrilled to hear his daughter was back in the states and staying put for awhile. She visited for some holidays and dragged him and his new wife out to tour western Pennsylvania once or twice.

Brink found Pittsburgh weirdly beautiful, it looked to her like the first modern ruin re-settled by futurists. She split her time between urban renewal projects and building a team of neuroscientists, a community of peers with whom she could finally get some rigorous work done.

Her first recruit, Mina Hasty, dreamed of building better bodies. His father was afflicted with a degenerative disease which eventually left him trapped inside an uncommunicative shell. Mina had an insatiable appetite for answers and smashed through problems as if she were wielding a hammer. Before her father died, Mina figured out how to transfer the relatively new brainwave remote-control technology into a humanoid chassis that her dad virtually inhabited momentarily. She solved a number of mysteries about the nervous system before she graduated.

Jello Green was the opposite of Mina. He was like a snaking stream, cutting through loose soil until he opened up the landscape and turned into a river. He was a warm voice of humanism in a department full of eager researchers who sometimes forgot the H came before the C. He lived in the chemical soup and electrical galaxy deep inside the mechanism of neurons, a cold dark region no one wanted to spend a lot of time in. He saw it as a colorful magical maelstrom and he kept everyone humbled by the vastness of the work they were doing.

Anderlos Dilg, a prodigy whom Brink considered an intellectual superior (which was fantastic fuel for her ambitions), was another brain artist. He worshipped Brink. He became head of the project, pun intended, for Google Hat, or Ghat, which brought the popularity of hat wearing back to the American populace and the internet into a non-invasive neural interface to whomever wore it. While working on this neural network project, in a warehouse full of supercomputers inside a giant faux pirate ship, Dilg begged Brink for guidance and support. He knew she knew things about the brain he never would, but she carefully avoided helping, herself highly dubious about the potential impacts of Ghat, though she did look deeply into it and that birthed new ambitions for her IMAC. When the project became ubiquitous around the globe and Brink started using data culled from it for her RECEP work, Dilg stopped speaking to her.

12 – ALL BRAINS ARE CREATED

Sulis was staring at what looked like a plate of spaghetti receiving shock treatment inside a tornado. In a smaller part of another screen was a yellow dot representing that maelstrom and it was moving north out of Athens.

There were other screens and chairs in the room, but none of the other technicians could concentrate because Sulis was prone to shout things like, "What in the holy fuck are you two doing now?" at least a few times a session.

Brink sent her updates when the original plan went sideways, but nothing since, and Sulis's impulse was to shut the whole thing down. The George incident didn't help.

George Papadimitriou felt a little nauseous under the warm sun as he wobbled from the metro towards his small apartment in the loud part of Metaxourgeio. He could swear he overheard pigeons speaking as they skittered away from him.

Lying in his bed four hours before he normally went to sleep, he listened to the color of his ceiling. He was thankful it wasn't speaking like the birds. It was humming. The sound was different from the grey wall which was unlike the buzz of his caramelizing skin. Nothing was adding up, so he got up and went back to the lab, broke in (though he had an entry code), curled up in the wire room against the chilled wall of the testing facility living quarters, and listened to the dull drone of the conversations inside.

The next morning, when Sulis went in to check for connection problems, she found the man she knew as the rude and hilarious server installer rocking gently to an unheard song, his clothes folded neatly on the floor beside him.

Sulis crouched next to him, checking his pupils, and softly repeated his name.

"Pós eísai?" he said, with the concern of a sage. Sulis immediately suspected foul play. Not by George, but by any of the innumerable parties interested in stealing, destroying, or generally opposing Brink's technology.

She was able to coax him to dress himself, but she couldn't figure out how to justify coaxing him into some testing. He lived alone, though he supported an estranged wife and child, had many friends, and passed all the requirements of employment. His contacts were reached and paramedics came to take him to the hospital.

Sulis desperately wanted to look into his mind.

13 – MULTIPLE HEART THEORY

Brink stretched her broad shoulders and craned her neck at the calm sky, pleasantly startled by Magic Man's opening wail as she waited for her bike's tank to fill at one of the few remaining petrol stations in the county. The night's tender but steady snowfall gave early morning Millvale a fresh mask, spring eagerly making plans underneath. Service vehicles went about their business silently. The station attendant gave her a wave, as usual, then seemed to disappear. The click of the stopped pump went unheard. She started to loosen her helmet to make sure there were still sounds in the world when the crunching roar of a recreational vehicle shattered the quiet.

The long side panel of the beast slid into Brink's vision. Emblazoned in black and lime and green and red against the huge chalky white vehicle was an illustration of dinosaurs arm-in-arm singing around a burning forest. Lettering below it read "Evolution Revolution" with tiny text underneath, "Science Education, UCSD."

The driver opened the door and stepped down, struggling a little to put on his jacket. He rubbed his arms with a shiver. "I forgot how warm I keep it in there," he said in a neighborly tone.

Brink, covered in exoskeletal polymers, chunky motorcycle duds, wasn't sure if she was reading female. She went a little blank, put her hand up and waved awkwardly.

The driver smiled, the mist of his warm exhale seemed to reach for her. "Nice bike," he said.

She ignored him, pretending to be preoccupied by returning the gas pump. Before she looked up again, he'd gone inside the convenience store. She leapt on her motorcycle and tore off, stopping a block away, heart pounding, close enough to see him come back out. She sat and watched him walk around his vehicle, checking tire pressure, cleaning windows, and doing various maintenance chores, as if she were watching an erotic film.

Eventually the lumbering chariot set out toward trees made fiery by sunrise. She was on her way to a meeting at U-PARC so she was a little surprised to find herself following the driver. Whoever was at the wheel of that nerd tank deserved a groupie. There was no way she was going to miss whatever show this guy put on. For sanity's sake, it only took a little over an hour for the first performance, Dreamboat Annie long over, the grooves forever the soundtrack to this inept stalking.

There's no real subtlety to following someone on a motorcycle across windy country roads but she did manage to stay out of sight when the students and teachers of Bechdel Elementary followed the evolution man out of the school to the lawn. Brink crouched in the woods across the street, risking ticks and shame.

The children appeared to be laughing. The teachers were smiling broadly. Evolution man was gesturing towards his ride with just enough Wonka-vibe creep to keep Brink's interest at a fever pitch. She never got a great look at that side of his ride, opposite the dinosaur illustration, but from a few views along the

74

ride, it appeared to be a provocative take on the last supper starring a collection of several of our extinct hominid cousins. This was confirmed when, some impassioned movement and inaudible speech later, the entire side panel opened like elevator doors. It would have looked sinister if not for the audible oohs and aahs throughout the class. Brink couldn't see what was being revealed. She fought the impulse to wander out of the woods like a voyeur zombie, and instead tried to figure out what they were seeing by reading their little faces. They seemed to be reacting to multiple people. Could he have an assistant in there? A significant other?

The lesson went on for an interminable twenty-five minutes, then he went back into the school alongside the chattering, flirty teachers followed as if in a trance by the glowingly entertained kids.

She ran at the RV, climbed on the driver's step and stared inside. A stack of magazines and journals. A cooler. An atrocious, adorable sweater. But no view into the back. It was closed and locked. He seemed to be taking his time, she thought, tapping the glass arrhythmically. There must be follow-up instruction going on inside. Thorough. She expected nothing less. One last weak pull on the door handle, then she pulled herself effortlessly onto the roof, hoping to find a skylight to look through or perhaps rip open. There were none. She did notice the texture of the roof was unusual, a material she couldn't identify with any confidence. Distracted with trying to figure out the alloy, she almost didn't notice the kids returning.

She heard his voice again and melted, considering life as a happy barnacle. Then the driver door opened. And the engine started. For the first time, Brink noticed the vehicle was electric.

The gas station must have fueled what was inside. Or did he even pump any gas? She got confused in a way she never had. Another distraction.

The kids shouted heartburstingly optimistic farewells as they walked alongside, until a small cluster of kids, who had all along been pointing at the top of the truck, spread the commotion to the whole group. The activity was conspicuous enough for the driver to notice they were no longer waving goodbye. He stopped.

Brink had no idea what was happening, her body stretched out, certain she'd kept out of view. It occurred to her that the moment they came out of the building, at least one set of keen eyes would have immediately cast upon the vehicle where they saw what probably looked like an incompetent ninja shuffling atop it. The wise thing to do in the situation was wait until evolution man got out, then roll over the driver side and slink away somehow. If she did manage to escape, would she keep up the sad shadowing? And what consequence to the kid or kids who really did see her? Would they become storytellers? Pariahs? Start a new religion?

She stood. She stood and put her hands up as if caught by an Old West Sheriff. Still wearing her bike armor with the matted mess of her long, milky purple hair covering half her face, the kids went wild. The driver noticed the teacher's faces, shocked and disappointed. Brink lowered herself over the front with a giant guilty smile. The driver couldn't believe what he was seeing and she couldn't believe she still could not see inside into the back compartment.

He calmly got out as Brink dismounted with pointless grace.

Without a look her way, he walked past, shoulders-out, and addressed the kids, "My assistant, who is a professional stuntwoman, wants to remind you how dangerous it is to travel on the outside of your timeship."

He looked imploringly at her. She took a moment to snap to and said, "That was a terrible idea. And dangerous. Never ever ride on top of any vehicle, especially when it's your beautiful, safe, warm ... time ... ship?"

She turned to get inside. He blocked her way. She whispered to him, breathlessly, "I must get inside."

"As punishment," he told the kids, "my assistant will be not be able to join me on future adventures."

He spoke to her under his breath, "Get on your bike and please drive away slowly and safely."

His fury made her drunk. And he'd noticed her following him!

She pretended to slump away and floated toward her bike. Vociferous protests broke out among the kids. The further away she got, the louder. The teachers couldn't tell if it was all part of the presentation. The man was about to explain when Brink turned around. She couldn't resist. Everyone got quiet as she walked into the middle of the crowd.

"None of you would ever do something so dangerous, would you?" she cried out.

"No!" replied most of the kids.

Brink turned towards the driver. "If I promise never to do something so foolish again, can I please come with you?"

The teachers seemed taken with the performance, assuming the science lesson came with a safety one as well.

With an expression Brink would never forget, the man pointed at the side door. She clapped her hands and bounded over. She had to stop herself from screaming out, "The time machine is mine!" Opening the door, she turned and waved, thanking the kids for their support.

The man shook hands with the two confused teachers, leapt aboard, and started away.

He stopped a few hundreds yards from the school and turned towards Brink, "If you'd like to get some lunch, I'll meet you up the road at Zhen's," then he stared at the passenger door.

14 – THE BLUE ANT

Sulis stared into the fake living room like a detective at a murder scene. The colors were browns and yellows and whites, utterly boring, but pleasant. A breakfast palette. There was a kitchen against the far wall, beige and marbled granite. It was functional and messy. It was mostly couches. The residents had been in there for almost two months. Sulis found the lighting unusual. It was warm, diffusive. Everything was fully illuminated, essentially shadowless, but it didn't look clinical. She wondered whether that effect was being considered.

The cohorts on her side of the glass were focused intently on their monitors, each spooling live information from the volunteers' brains, every connection, every chemical trigger, every wave dancing like a crazed electrical circus run by mad magicians.

Sulis wandered around the control room, stopping at Anatole's station.

"This is one of those subjects, yeah?" Sulis asked, pointing at the three behind the glass and a tangle on a screen.

"It is," Anatole said, as the techs gathered to see what she was looking at.

"That is Nerida. The others Effie and Spiro. Anatole watch Effie, yes?" Niko said.

Sulis looked back and forth at the screen while Effie stood holding open the refrigerator door, the telltale look of the lackadaisical hunter.

"Oh. Oh wow," Anatole said. "I don't look at these regions so much. Nice. Good catch."

"I'm sorry," Sulis said, turning towards the staff. "It's nice to meet you all."

"Don't be silly," another research assistant said pulling her chair up to Anatole's desk. "Is incredible. I'm Gloria," she said, quickly shaking hands with Sulis.

The team were looking at a rampant growth of connections in various regions of Effie's brain far out of pace with normal activity.

"Is she creative? Has she had any injuries lately? Have you seen anything like this before from any of them?" Sulis asked like an insurance officer processing a claim. "Let me know if you want me to butt out."

"She has a four-year-old girl her mother is caring for," Anatole explained. "Had a bank job for a few months. Laid off. No creative pursuits she's shared or displayed so far."

"There's nothing weird in the frig?" Sulis asked.

Anatole brought up a camera view so they could all see inside.

"You can see she's spaced out and not from salami," Paval said.

"It could be salami," Gloria said.

"We should set up a portal," Niko advised.

"Of course, yes," Anatole said, enthusiastically setting up the program.

It turned out there were problematic regions in Effie's frontal lobe.

"Please tell me that's not what it looks like," Sulis said, closing her eyes.

"Cannot be."

"It can be. We need contrast," Gloria said.

"We can see here these aren't glial cells. We're good. Well, she's good. I'm more concerned if there's a relationship to George's condition. Have you had a chance to run him through testing?" said Sulis.

"Something very strange is still going on here, even if it isn't cancer-related," said Gloria.

"Yes, you're exactly right," Sulis added. "Boss lady been vocal lately?"

"Not at all. As you see, they're having a bit of a mess in there."

They all cocked their heads looking at Leopold's readouts, as if looking together added their intelligences together.

"I'm on it," Sulis yelped, rushing to her console.

15 – THE ONE AND ONLY EM

The summer rain hid them from the guilt of doing nothing. Brink rested her large feet on Shelby's warm lap, each interrupting the other's reading every few sentences.

"Wait, how was she planning on getting that done? Did she expect you to do it all along?"

"You're trying to make me cry?"

"Baby, I'm sorry, of course not. I meant, you know what I meant."

Brink smiled, but he could see her at the edge of tears.

"I've not spent any time thinking about what she would have done, that's a little troubling. Is it troubling?"

Shelby put his book down and rubbed her feet and said carefully, "Can you tell I'm not sold on the idea?"

Brink was silent for a moment, put her book down, then turned her hips and snuggled against his chest. "Yeah, I wasn't trying to sell it, but that's the part I'd suck at anyway. Are you bothered by the general ongoing fear and rejection of metanarratives in the soft arts, the valiant feminist battle with it, or the unbeatable competition of mythos?"

"All of the above, plus a lot. Mainly though, how do you avoid helping dictators who always see the story of human achievement paving the way to them?"

"How do you avoid manifest destiny think?"

"Yeah, and that."

"You can't avoid it. But like, imagine you're doing your thing with the kiddos and they hit you with the religious questions..."

"Every time."

"Right, so instead of hitting them with counterfactuals, you co-opt their story because it's the exact same story, only the characters and locations and power dynamics are in fact factual. Ruining Santa Claus doesn't take the fun out of Christmas, it lets you in on making Santa Claus fun for the little-os who don't know yet. The only problem in this endeavor is the authority game. The power dynamics. If the administration at whichever school wasn't cool with evolution being taught in the first place, you ain't gettin' to those kids."

"So you're saying you gotta have Empires. And they send it down from on high, by force if necessary?"

"You're such a dude."

"Are you okay?" Shelby asked with a face Brink hadn't seen yet.

"Yes, of course, I love talking about her."

"I"m glad to hear that, but not what I mean."

Brink shivered a little and her countenance changed.

"Yeah, see, this is you, where did you go there?"

"Are you serious?"

"Don't get upset ..." Shelby said, regretting the words.

"I'm not, love. I'm blown away. You could tell?"

Shelby scrunched up his face. "You weren't you there for a minute is all. I mean you were there and talking but I don't know, it was strange."

Brink's face got big. "I have to tell you something. Wait, why am I telling you?"

Shelby grabbed her as if she were leaving. She leaned close to his face, gave him a short soft kiss and said, "I have a superpower that no one has ever noticed before and it freaked me out that you might have just noticed. Real appropriate wash of guilt I think."

"Stop fucking with me. That was kind of unnerving. What's with this superpower nonsense. You don't talk like this when we're in serious mode."

"When did we hit serious mode?! Oh, because we're talking about my mom?"

"Love, I take it back, I'm still a little high."

Brink took a little breath.

"Not sure how to explain this. I don't have a dissociative disorder, but I can do a couple things in my noggin 'consciously' at the same time."

Shelby leaned back to get a good view of her face. "I don't get it."

"Back when I mentioned never thinking about what my mother would get up to if she didn't die, I started thinking about that."

"While you were talking to me?"

"Yeah."

"Bullshit."

"I am happy to verify my party tricks for you any time, squinty."

"You're saying you were able to go autopilot and talk to me while contemplating something else in your head, like you weren't paying any attention to our conversation? Like a sound trick?"

"Not at all, I was totally, well, as you noticed, almost totally, with you. You must have noticed because I was far more focused on the mom stuff and also something like, you love me?"

"You're very lucky I love you."

She leapt on his lap. "I know!"

"But I'm not done with this. Is it like singing and reading two different things at the same time?"

"Yeah, exactly like that but not at all the same."

She could see he still felt a little abandoned. She put her forehead on his. "Baby, let me put it this way. I have a hard time seeing people and things as people and things because I opened a few too many doors en mi cabeza, but you are the most real thing in the world to me and you make me feel whole."

She could see the weight in his eyes.

"And I owe you a better explanation for le grand empirical metanarrative!"

Brink stood up and swung her ass around towards him, wearing his light blue boxers and his red t-shirt. She bent over, grabbed her tablet, did a quick search, Shelby resisted reaching out for her.

"You ever read Slaughterhouse Five?"

"I think they showed us one of the movies in school? That's where they burn the books?"

"Oh no no, I mean things burn, but no."

"Oh shit, right that's the other one," Shelby said.

"There is a bit right at the beginning, I'll read it:

Over the years, people I've met have often asked me what I'm working on, and I've usually replied that the main thing was a book about Dresden.

"Oh yeah, the Vonnegut one, the World War."

"Shush!" Brink commanded.

I said that to Harrison Starr, the movie-maker, one time, and he raised his eyebrows and inquired, "Is that an anti-war book?"

"Yes," I said. "I guess."

"You know what I say to people when I hear they're writing anti-war books?"

"No. What *do* you say, Harrison Starr?"

"I say, 'Why don't you write an anti-*glacier* book instead?'"

What he meant, of course ...

"Stop staring at my tits. This is the bit..."

What he meant, of course, was that there would always be wars, that they were as easy to stop as glaciers. I believe that, too.

And even if wars didn't keep coming like glaciers, there would still be plain old death.

"That was published in the 1960s and at the time, you'd have been thought of as nuts or quite dim to disagree," Brink said, sitting back on Shelby's lap. She nuzzled into his hard crotch. "I don't know if you've noticed but even though war still exists, and plain ol' death is a permanent feature, the reign of male problem solving techniques is on the way out. A creation story that we all share isn't a hard, inflexible tool for flourishing superpowers to rationalize their imperial transgressions," Brink said as she pulled the elastic of Shelby's shorts under his balls.

"If you ever pull that dual brain shit with me when we make love, I'll end you."

"End me, my love. Please end me."

16 – TIME TO INFORM THE BOSS

"I'm beefing up the security," said Sulis

"This looks like it's entirely on our end."

"I don't care. You are wrong all the time."

"Rude!"

"Also ..."

"More rude!"

"Definitely also, please tell me you've noticed your son screwing up his connection causing a full on schema break in the semantic console."

"I was obviously dangerously late to discovering but yes, I'm working on a plan, boss."

Sulis couldn't help but pee a little at being called Boss, even humorously, by Brink herself.

"Are you guys good?" Sulis asked.

"Stay tuned! I think I gotta go kill a philosopher."

Sulis kept her comm open well past Brink signing off.

Brink abruptly popped back on, "Oh, right right. Do NOT let those volunteers go anywhere. Put Fenix on it if you have to."

"Will do, mom. Oh for fuck's sake, I'm sorry."

"Love you, darling. Gotta go. Brush your teeth!"

17 – BREATHE

Shelby could tell he was being rude letting her do all the talking but he couldn't help it. It just got better and better.

"My mom created me as a big fuck you to the rich."

"She didn't create you, I mean, you call her mom."

"Yes, she's my dear loving mother, right, but. There was a whole lot of Frankensteining that went on to get me looking and walking and breathing and speaking and the lot. The 'displaying consciousness' bit was the easy part."

BREATHE

The vehicle started out crowded, but Brink's equipment had grown to cover every unused space in the RV. Brink was trying, for the three or four hundredth time, to convince Shelby to let her experiment on his kids. Shelby found it charming though eventually the bit got stale when he figured out she was serious. He was concerned she wasn't keeping up with her work which seemed to rely on a lot of the equipment jostling around in the cab most of the time and that she did too much to help him advance his own solar cellular work. Brink was quite active with a lot of new designing, a favorite part of any project, and she even tried to keep up her CMU work, quite happy Dilg had gone fully private.

"Did you know that Supergirl dated her horse?!" Brink burst out the non sequitur almost on schedule. Shelby loved them because it invited him into multiple paths of reality. Either he was about to get laid, he was about to be intellectually pummeled, or he was about to geek out, so many happy avenues lit up.

A hard rap rattled the inside of the vehicle. Shelby threw a shirt on and opened the door. Two young men loitered several paces behind a third who, with stiff arm rested on the RV, leaned his head in as if being surreptitious about having a look inside.

"What y'all got going on here?"

"You want to come in?" Shelby said.

"Iin think so. You from Pennsylvania?"

"California."

"An you'n think we come from monkeys?"

Brink stood out of sight, coiled like a snake, watching for cues in the muscles of Shelby's face.

The visitor answered for himself, "I reckon we do. I seen em in the zoo acting more like a person then most my family, knowwhatimsayin?" He laughed. Shelby did too. "You work with kids?" He asked, pointing at the artwork.

"Yep, science education," Shelby said.

"Good. We need that round here. Good. Look, I didn't mean to bother y'all. I never seen a vehicle like this," he said, caressing its solar skin.

"Well, you know, the real project is the rig - she's coated in a new solar paint and we're testing it. Doing some science education for the kids along the way is just the fun part."

Shelby went outside to tell the gentleman and his companions all about the technology. Brink followed her naive, adorable sugarplum from window to window as they circled the RV swapping stories. Turned out two of the guys were unemployed electrical engineers.

There was a bottle thrown in anger at their symbolic ride here and there, a death threat in this or that forum, but resistance to what they were peddling was far less than they expected, or at least what Brink had expected.

As the only representative in the history of life on earth of her peculiar phenotype, it was always bemusing to Brink that she still got caught up in the grotesque nonsense of racism, that she sometimes inspired fear, but mostly the mundane shuffling superiority of lazy bigotry.

Weirdly, it was far worse in Arizona than the Midwest, but Brink figured that was long-lingering British manners, those self-satisfying kindnesses that are more ownership than connection.

BREATHE

They'd spent almost a year in blissful adventure across the southern landscape. They'd successfully avoided being the subject of popular press, though they featured in a number of journals and international papers.

After a body-numbingly delicious meal in Austin, Texas, while discussing their future, Shelby's tone went serious.

"Baby, you know I love you."

"Uh oh," Brink said, shrinking.

"Far be it from me to doubt anything you do, let alone understand most of what you do, but I've noticed you are spread pretty thin."

"How so?"

"The bed is covered with books and pads, half of which display patiently waiting chat partners about subjects I'm pretty sure have nothing to do with each other," Shelby said.

"Is this an intervention?"

"You're so good at letting others deal with defending your patents, managing your IP, running your businesses, but what ever happened to your dream of starting a school?"

"At least one of those screens is dedicated to that, I'm sure."

"Or finishing that mad project of your mother's?"

Brink made a guilt-filled "oh that" face.

"What I'm saying is we should really be thinking about what comes next," Shelby said, his posture and intonation softening.

Brink felt the world shift. Electric shot up the hair along her spine. Shelby kicked the chair out from underneath him and dropped a knee.

"It doesn't matter what you're doing, as long as you're doing it with me. Marry me, my perfect love."

Shelby pulled a napkin out of his shirt pocket and unwrapped a ring molded from a twist of octopus limb. Brink had raved about it in a shop several thousand miles ago.

"You want?" he said with his irresistible smile.

Brink dropped her head, "I don't know. One man. One woman. Seems a little old fashioned."

He lifted her chin with his other hand. Her eyes were full of tears. She burst out of her seat, leaping over the table and tackling him, screaming "Yes!" The restaurant patrons clapped and whistled as she attacked him. "Give it to me already," she cried, and he slipped the ring on her finger.

"I should have done this before the meal," he said, pretend straining beneath her, though there were bruises.

{{{{{ BREATHE }}}}}

Over the next few days, Brink found herself distracted by thoughts of dedication, ceremony, and children. The real complications with children. Another fun work challenge, she thought, whenever she needed a giggle. She was tempted to continue the trend with half of her mind while she got back to work with the other, but it was too curious. She wasn't that far from being a normal person, but she'd never been one for ritual and thought she was immune. She grew quickly addicted to the happy chemicals of purposeful monogamy. Even his mother's serious doubts about her qualifications as a human didn't bother her. Buying her a house didn't hurt.

"Arjun, he asked me to marry him," was the first thing she said when Arjun answered her call.

"The solar boy?"

"Solar man, thank you."

"I like him."

"That's it?"

"You're almost 30, right?"

"I'm almost 20!"

Arjun was quiet. Maybe she heard a slight exhale.

"Your mother got married too young also. I'll prepare a prenup."

"Bitter old man."

"It's wonderful, little thing. I'm very happy for you. You two are a perfect team. I'm playing," said Arjun. "Though I will send you the prenup by Wednesday."

"You're so gross. How's *your* better half?"

"Saoirse is excellent, thank you. She'll be over the moon by the news. She'll also point out jealously that you are far too young. But she doesn't know you were an old man by the time you were four, a teenage girl by seven, and some kind of extra-planetary space monster by puberty."

"I really love this boy," Brink purred.

"Man."

"I'm so excited. It's ridiculous."

"When and where are we doing this?"

"Doing what?"

"The wedding."

"Oh, I can't just be in this dopamine drip of list making forever?"

"I'm for it."

"I love you, Arjundad."

"Not nearly as much as I love you."

Brink's eyes were full of tears.

"Oh, you've got it bad," Arjun said, shaking his head.

"I know," Brink said, holding back sobs and laughter. "Bye!"

NEVER STOP BREATHING

They'd been looking forward to Memphis. Shelby was careful never to drink the night before a presentation, so they took a few days to enjoy the music and bars in town. And then, all of a sudden it seemed, after nearly two years on the road, there were only a few stops left before their wildly successful tour was done. Shelby took Brink to a park in Nashville with the promise of a unique picnic.

When he unfurled the tartan throw onto the short grass, Brink was surprised to find herself sitting down to a romantic lunch in front of the Parthenon, or at least the full size replica built in the nineteenth century for a state centennial expo. The theme of the meal was the future. Shelby pitched an idea. For our next trick, how about we travel the world together, working on your mom's dream of bringing the empirical meta-narrative to the people, he said to her adoring wide-eyed gaze. It was perfect. She saw her whole life and it was beautiful.

Then she woke up. And there was fire. She was bleeding. And being torn from a collapsed section of the RV, flames choking her, the dark night and searing heat making her blind. A fire engine's screaming siren was at the edge of her hearing. There were tight grips on her arms and torso, highway patrolman dragging her away from her burning home. She squeezed her stinging eyes, slowly gathering clarity. The men's tones were reassuring, but sounded the opposite. One held her as she coughed and wheezed. The other brought water. Brink finally got her eyes open and saw the conflagration. The entire front section of the vehicle was a cauldron of orange and black. Brink shot forward but her body was weak and the officer held firm. She threw her arm back aimlessly, broke his clavicle, and sped towards the inferno. The officers bolted after her, another one close behind, screaming "We have him, ma'am! Over here!" Brink halted, almost falling over, spun around, spitting, "Where?!"

The officers all shook their heads. She considered turning back around, but it was clear what their expressions meant. She collapsed, sobbing. The officers approached slowly, even the injured one. Each tried to offer a hand, but were startled when Brink suddenly leapt up and raced towards the ambulance. There was a gurney inside, covered in a slightly smoldering blanket in the shape of the love of her life. The other officers caught up when paramedics and new officers tried to keep her from entering the ambulance. They called them off, convincingly.

Brink leaned close to where she thought his head was. She choked and sputtered, "Darling! My love! I'm here!" She delicately tried to remove the blanket but an EMT put his hand in the way, firmly saying, "He was severely burned, you'll only make it worse."

18 – HAUNTED BY LONG WALKS

The shallow canyon wind made him feel cold. He kept being surprised his sensory skin still worked so well here. At the same time, he was amused to find he now instinctively blamed natural phenomena on local gods. The girl seemed unaffected by the weather. For hours and hours, he'd been the quiet recipient of the most exclusive ethnographic tour of all time as she made even the smallest blue flower along the trodden butter-colored dirt the hero of a grand superhuman tale. Though who knows how accurate any of this was now, thought Leopold. He was having all kinds of thoughts because, fugchucks, this was a long walk.

They encountered very few other travelers, even when near small villages. When it was close to dark, the girl, who had never been to this part of the world, kept them off the well-trod path when possible, and found a secluded meadow at the base of a massive rock shaped a bit like a tent.

She said they'd avoided the crossroads where poor King Oedipus killed his father.

"Have you heard the true story of Oedipus and Sphinx," she asked as she tidied the area and laid down their bedrolls.

Creon, King of Thebes, had promised the throne to whomever could solve her riddle, so Oedipus and Sphinx hatched a plan.

Sphinx had told Oedipus the answer secretly, at night, during one of their naughty meetings. When he gave the right answer, she'd fly away screeching and crying that she'd end her life, but would come back when he sent for her and hide in his chambers forever. The next day, when he stood at the gate, in front of everyone, and she growled and spat the riddle, it was a different form than everyone had heard before, including Oedipus. He was terrified. Had the answer changed? Was his lover as devious and cruel as everyone said? Sure, she devoured all who couldn't answer the question, but that was her job. He loved her. He wanted her. But doubt crept into his heart. His throat became raw. The crowd cheered him. Mothers looked away. He gave her his trust. He gave the answer. She scowled, showed her horrible teeth. Then she spread her wings, lashed her serpent tail like a whip, and lifted angrily into the sky. She flew away in circles, looking back to watch her love bask in the glory of his compatriots.

Leopold found himself leaning forward, mouth open.

"Sphinx watched from the mountains that night, her keen eyes warmed by the torches inside the room of the new hero. Everyone thought she'd gone off to die, as was told. Instead, she waited, silently, hunting small prey to stay alive over the long years. Oedipus grew to a man. She was thin and starving when he at last took the throne. She waited and watched. But Oedipus had forgotten about her. He never called for her. Some say she let herself die, let herself waste away to feed the worms. But some of us know she is still out here, bitter and old, waiting for a new lover," the girl paused, moved closer to Leopold, made her eyes large, and said "to eat!" jumping at him.

Leopold laughed after he startled. He could not believe he'd fallen for a twenty-five-hundred-year-old campfire story.

Eventually the girl fell into a deep sleep. Leopold laid down next to her to block the wind, though he was sad his body couldn't provide much warmth. He eventually felt the night call him and he got some much needed rest.

19 – THE FORMER L.A.

She screamed at the never-black Los Angeles night, her legs warmed by the Mustang's growling hood. The tequila was coming back up. She could convince no one to risk arrest. It was the last day the river would be a prisoner of concrete. It was hard to find anyone still willing to race her, her death wish like a spectral passenger everyone could see tugging at her wheel. She fell asleep pissing herself a few strides from a porta-potty.

The next thing Brink knew she was squinting at the rising desert sun in the backseat of someone else's car, her head resting on a girl's lap she did not recognize. She adjusted to the grey morning light by focusing on the girl's pert breasts and the t-shirt design racing around them, vines and tubes and wires, luscious thick and thin lines swirling around letters. She shot up, almost colliding with the snoozing girl's chin. Brink grabbed her shoulders and turned her torso towards her.

"What's wrong?" the girl said, still half asleep. "Are we getting out?"

"Are you supposed to be following me?"

The girl felt the tone more than she heard the words and tried to pull out of Brink's grip. "Let go of me," she said.

Brink complied, her mind racing to reconstruct her situation. "Where did you get that shirt?"

"It's mine," the girl said.

"I don't care whose it is. Where did you get it?"

The conversation's tone reached the front seat.

"Hey, you two. What is going on back there?" said the passenger with a peculiarly masculine French accent.

The thick-necked Frenchman, the skinny-cute driver, the big-eyed girl, Brink recognized no one.

"Where are we going?" she asked.

The passenger laughed. "Back to hotel. Se laver pour le travail. Non? Ton français travillaint hier soir. How you feeling?"

She felt fine. That's what she'd been telling herself for months.

She didn't remember how she arrived at Taer's doorstep, but she remembered how kind she was. After Brink's worrying paralysis on the antique chaise, Taer hired a live-in caregiver whom Brink did her best to corrupt. Taer's friends dropped by regularly to make tea, bring food, help with bathing, and get high. Old colleagues were alerted. Psychologists recommended. A surfeit of futile heartbreak cure. An accidental shiva performed. After thirty days, grief being a timed biological mechanism, Brink rose from bed. Taer's Laurel Canyon home was like a tinderbox to Brink's smoldering need for companionship. At first, Taer enjoyed having young people around.

She looked back at the girl and bowed her head in apology. "I'm a little sick."

"Need to pull over?" the driver asked, sweetly.

"I'm good. Thanks though."

The girl put her hand on Brink's forehead, brushed her hair away. She brought Brink back onto her lap and kissed the top of her head.

The kiss brought it back. She did find a race, someone agreed to race to Vegas but she ran out of charge somewhere along the cold desert. The winner gave her a ride to a party in Henderson. That's where this trio were, enjoying themselves, and casually recruiting for what they described was Peace Corps meets Habitat for Humanity meets polyamory. She wasn't sure if she was too high when she noticed they all wore the same tight black shirt emblazoned with the garland themed logo made up of the letters T, W and F. They told her their chapter was three months old, that they were all kind of flailing around in life before committing to the cause, and were excited how fast it was growing. She's not sure what happened after that, but was surprised to find she was still with them.

More surprising was she seemed to be agreeing to approach what appeared to be a random suburban front door. Brink lodged herself in a random stucco recess, listening intently, confused as hell. A welcome feeling, she thought.

"Good evening. Joined up with the TWF yet?"

"Oh no no. No, thank you. Good night," said the woman who answered the door.

"You heard of us?" The burly cute boy asked firmly.

"Of course, yes. My husband is NOT a fan."

"There are still a lot of guys scared of women with power."

"Oh, I'm one of them," the married woman said while looking up and down the handsome TWF star. "Last thing we need are female leaders."

And with that line, the gang turned to walk away. It's one of the rules.

Not aware of any of these rules, Brink stepped angrily from the dark towards the woman, who looked more than startled.

"Please don't hurt me," she cried, folding in to herself.

"Oh no, sweetie, I'm so sorry. That angry wasn't for you. Forgive me. Your husband, on the other hand," Brink said with as much humor she could summon.

Brink's fantastical, uniquely charming smile punched through the married woman's fear and skepticism and she laughed.

Brink turned back to the pros, "DO you guys have, like, literature to give out?"

"We certainly do," the back seat girl said, brandishing The Lil Purple Pamphlet. The French dude quickly injected, "We are by the community for the community. Our main goal is to end loneliness, increase happiness, and end hunger. But we do all kinds of fun support stuff. This guy," he said presenting the hunky guy, "is our best masseur. And he's free. Crazy busy, but he serves the cause like I do. Well, a little like I do."

"And we have super cute badges and if you get more involved, all kinds of fun uniforms," said backseat girl and she handed the pamphlet to the receptive married woman.

"Are y'all sex workers?" the married woman barely got out of her throat.

Brink spun around. "Are you?!" she whispered.

The clear leader of the group, the backseat girl, said, "We're a community organization dedicated to healing, to repairing what's broken, and nurturing what needs nurturing, which includes human touch, human voice," she paused, gathering strength, looked at Brink with awe and desire, "and superhuman presence?"

"They are trying to recruit me too," Brink said to the married woman, who winked at Brink.

"Oh, I thought you were their boss. You're quite imposing," the married woman said, not aware of how obvious the flirtation was.

The sexy dude piped up, "We must get to a thorough scrubbing of a wastewater treatment plant. Would you like to join us?"

"What is your name, beautiful?" Brink asked the married woman.

"Trish. Can I...?" Trish said, holding up a video ball.

Brink complied warmly. Trish held her strong body with a thrill. Brink smiled and gave her a quick peck on the head.

"Thank you all for a real interesting evening. I gotta make dinner but good luck with your project. I'll check on it I swear."

"Wonderful meeting you, Trish. Have a fun night," Brink said, then winked.

They arrived at an inexpensive hotel far from the Strip, among the ramshackle homes most affected by the water sanctions. They were meeting up with a few more potential recruits and installing solar cells, dry farming, and giving the odd massage. Brink spent the day with them, sweating, laughing. She took a moment to find a quiet place where she broke down sobbing, her head to the ground.

The group had made a dozen new friends, and Brink expected many of those would join the cause.

"Are you interested? There are a lot of groups in LA. That's where it started, we think," the cute driver said. Their recruitment techniques were surprisingly sophisticated.

"Of course, yes. I'm in," Brink replied. She couldn't believe how Taer managed to resist revealing the author. "I guess mystery cult leaders work better?" she thought.

They exchanged details, Brink using the nom de plume she'd gone by all day, Josie Jetson . Brink excused herself from the evening's celebrations, surreptitiously called a cab, then flew back to Burbank.

Brink came swinging in to the top floor chill space and was only slightly astounded to see the Governor of California in her loveseat.

"Yeah, that's my, uh, ya know," Brink teased.

105

The Governor stood up immediately to embrace her. Brink looked uncharacteristically impressed and returned to hug.

"Hey you know how humans don't have estrus?"

The governor was reduced to a giddy child, jumping to the conclusion that Brink was hitting on her and she couldn't hide her thrill. She quickly composed herself. She was here on serious business.

"Eye dilation, voice modulation which I heard climbing up a fucking tree as you discussed looking forward to meeting me with a real flirt, and need I point out your hips currently?"

"Do NOT be rude, young lady," Taer shouted at her stepdaughter, trying to hold back a giggle, her political friend quite obviously melting.

"Yeah, you. I came home ready to make you an 'I'm so damn proud of you meal', instead the Governor is in my chair. What's up, girls? Since when does the TWF do politics?"

Both of them guffawed, shocking Brink.

"Honey, not only is there right now a twiffer city councilwoman, look who is currently our most powerful member," Taer announced proudly.

"Please tell me you're joking."

"It's really an alliance of the Green Party rolled into ..."the Governor tried to explain.

"About calling themselves that," Brink clarified with weirdly out-of-place negativity.

Taer laughed, "Nicknames make themselves."

"Are you nuts telling the Governor of California I'm the source of the Feminesto?"

"That's the best part of the story. A seven-year-old shredding the concept of genius, creating the ultimate rallying cry for Feminine Superiority and creating a safe home for female rage ... I mean COME ON, who else in history could have done that other than your mom's daughter."

"Sweetie, I keep a lot of secrets," the Governor said, calmly. "You never have to worry about me."

"I don't mind you knowing of course. Or anyone. But so far, Taer's been able to lead and shape this baby without me lifting a finger and I'm gonna need that for a while longer."

"This is when Arjun would tell a really bad Ganesh joke," Taer said, shocking Brink.

Brink rushed into Taer's arms. The hug was deep and endless and melted Taer. She began to cry with Brink, who laughed as she wiped her own tears away.

"My poor thing," said Taer.

"Do not call this precious miracle a thing!" the governor said, utterly clueless to their dynamic.

"I'm going to finish it for you," Brink said, her voice garbled with sniffles.

"What is going on, darling?"

"The project mom hijacked. Are you still interested?"

Taer's eyes lit up. In an instant, she looked young again.

"Most of those rich bastards are still alive right?"

"What are you talking about?" Taer asked, pretending to hide her excitement.

"I spent the day with a gang of do-gooders who said they belonged to a Las Vegas chapter of the TWF. They also called themselves twiffers, for god's sake."

"Oh, honey, that has taken on a life of its own," Taer said, looking nervous.

"No. No, it was amazing. It was surreal. I'm incredibly proud of you."

"Be proud of yourself, little one," said the Governor, who shot a wide-eyed gaze at Taer and mouthed, 'it's true, I know it is now.'

Taer returned a shrug and a wink.

"You know what is now?" asked Brink.

"The Honorable Governor thought I might have been joking about you creating the TWF feminesto."

"Aw, so I had a chance to deny being involved?" Brink said. "Let's start over."

Brink turned back to Taer. "I know you're making a good living from consulting and it looks like the commercial TWF stuff is growing, but I know how much that project meant to you. I want to return the favor. Mom and I owe you one. I've decided to start my school here and our first project is your creepy life extension business. Are you in?"

Brink could see Taer's eyes light up simultaneously with hearts and dollar signs, as if she were the chimera of proud parents.

20 – NOT THIS PYTHIA, THANK YOU

The girl's tone changed the closer they got to their destination. She spoke of the job she was being prepared to do and it sounded like a way to deal with her nerves about it. Leopold figured it was stage fright or something. The tale sounded like yet another impossible story, until she went into detail. A visitor to the oracle, and there were up to three when business was booming, would bring dedications in the form of treasure and a sacrifice, then put questions to the priests. Those priests would think about the questions, prepare answers, then feed them to the pythia. She would deliver the answer ritually, sitting atop a high tripod. She would have sounded a little woozy, affected by the vapors that rose from a crevasse beneath the navel under her seat.

Leopold was lost and asked, "I'm hearing you say navel. What is a navel here?"

The girl gave Leopold yet another incredulous face, shook her head, then excitedly answered, "Zeus sent two eagles from the opposite edge of the world and the navel is where they met. My seat is at the center of the universe."

She continued, explaining that for a long time, only women of advanced years had been pythia due to the abuse suffered by the young, pretty girls, but she was sent to experiment with a new business model. Regardless of age, she said most in the position didn't last very long. She went on and on and it got darker and darker so that by the time they walked up the hill into the channel walls of the temple entrance in Delphi itself, Leopold thought it was the last place either of them should be. The place was creepy.

Two thickly wrapped old men approached Leopold with a jangling bag. Their eyes were on the girl. She increased her pace, excited to be greeted by holy men. Leopold tried to grab her hand but she deftly avoided him. The men tossed the bag to the ground in front of Leopold and turned to leave, ushering the girl in front of them. Leopold almost forgot he was wearing a classic Greek face, and cast a glare that pierced even the dark hearts of the old men. They turned away.

Leopold stood frozen until he noticed he was doing nothing. He started back to Athens.

Brink was reassured to find that he'd stopped in Delphi, then confounded, but delighted, when he almost immediately turned back.

She and the man who thought he owned her had woken early and made up some distance between the traveling parties. Leopold had already come all the way back to within a few hundred yards of them, at the place where the mountains spilled into the valley path.

Brink was forced to make a quick decision. She sprinted toward the slaver, leapt up his back, and twisted his head just so. He fell to the ground in a heap, unconscious. She had timed her escape poorly, caught up as she was in the imminent reunion. Leopold had witnessed the event at a great distance. He saw a man collapse, then the woman responsible running toward him. This instinctively made him back up, and start to retract his legs, but he caught himself. It might have been a woman in need as opposed to a woman who turns into a monster, so he waited. But the woman was running shockingly fast, and the shape of her was a bit odd, long arms, odd-sized feet. When she began waving and shouting, still unintelligible, Leopold pulled his legs up and rose slowly into the air. By the time he heard the words "Leopold! Wait!" he was hovering forty feet above her.

"Brink?" he cried.

"Brink!" he shouted almost angrily as he swooped down. At pace, he slammed into her chest with a pile-driving hug, lifting her into the air. She made an awful sound, struggling to breathe and laugh at the same time.

"What is going on?" Leopold shouted at her. He let them down not far from the unconscious man, and went on, "Who is that? Did you kill him? Was he trying to hurt you? Where have you been? Did you survive the wave? How did you find me? Where are we and why are we here and why didn't you warn me?" He paused for less than a second and concluded with "I need your help with a girl."

"I must say I did not see that last one coming," she said, feeling weirdly proud that the boy was still relatively sane considering the odd adventure he'd likely been on.

"There's a girl back there. I was just in this weird little city in the hills. Delphi. As in the Oracle of Delphi. I delivered a girl there to these freaky old weirdos. We have to get her out of there."

"Delivered?"

"Yes. It's not that far. I'll fly us."

"You did what now?"

"I didn't even realize what I was doing. I pretty much transferred an innocent girl from one prison to another."

"Popular business," Brink said motioning at the slumbering deliveryman.

"He kidnapped you?"

"Bought me."

Brink walked them to the man and said, "I have an idea. Fly back there and wait for me. But do not get seen flying. When you approach, hide in the hill above the temple. You know where I mean, right? The cliff. Out of sight. You'll see when you get there."

Leopold looked confused.

"This guy will take me into the heart of the place and we'll be in a much better position for a rescue. Plus, there's something I really have to check out in the pythia's chamber."

"That's what she called herself. A pythia."

"The little girl?"

"Yeah."

"I thought they were older ladies by this time. Wow, Leopold, you met a ..."

She was interrupted by a low groan. The man was waking up.

"What will you tell him happened? Are you sure you'll be okay?" Leopold asked.

"Get going, quick!" she said, poking at the sky.

Leopold went straight up as the man opened his eyes to find Brink crouched suppliantly in front of him. The man scowled, then clapped Brink across the head, knocking her over. Leopold looked down from high above, ready to descend violently on the man. Brink stood up quickly, head down, continuing her act of obedience, more for Leopold's sake, to indicate she was fine. She stretched her head and neck, pointing in the direction Leopold should be heading.

The man pulled a rope from his bag and tied Brink's arms behind her. Without a word he pushed her out in front of him and they continued on. Leopold followed directly above until they were well inside the mountain pass, then zigzagged off, convinced Brink knew what she was doing.

Leopold crept to the edge of the precipice above the temple, staring down at the walls of Delphi from a vantage point rare to its many illustrious, perspective-seeking visitors. He fought the urge to climb down and look for a window to peek through, mainly because it looked like there wasn't one.

He waited, spending almost an hour thinking of what he'd ask Brink. Thinking of how the IMAC could possibly work this well but also so wrong. Thinking of what they would do next if it was so dangerous. Thinking if this was a simulation, whether he could change stuff by concentrating really hard. But mostly thinking of Sulis. He missed his wonderful girlfriend.

The sun made one last golden stare from behind the western slopes before it fell away. Leopold saw two hikers approaching. It was Brink, scanning the hill for him. He fought the urge to wave. She didn't. Her captor had untied her before taking the winding paths up to the temple. It wouldn't look good if he had to deliver her in bonds. She pretended she understood, no hijinks. The delivery boy had to look good to get paid. Leopold watched them disappear into a building next to the main temple, or at least what he thought was the main temple. It was the biggest structure with all paths leading to it. From above, all the rectangular roofs looked the same.

Now there was a whole new, stressful stretch of time to kill. What could possibly be going on in there? How would Brink get in touch again? Would he have to wait all night? He couldn't wait anymore. He descended on the main temple, dropped over the side of the roof, floated between two columns, and hovered under the ceiling of the portico.

He heard footsteps approaching. They shuffled and multiplied. Leopold poked his head around the corner, staring down the stoa, the covered, columned walkway. Three elaborately draped older men, perhaps including the two from earlier, he couldn't tell, each wore headgear that obscured their faces. They were escorting the girl towards the entrance of the temple. Leopold did the best he could to hide in the shadows. Young boys, carrying silver trays that held an oddly burning substance, preceded them. It lit their path, sending even, blue light to every corner of the walkway. It made Leopold clearly visible, but they were too busy opening the large doors of the temple to notice him. Leopold slipped in as if he were a balloon they dragged behind. He had never skulked like this when flying before. The maneuvering wasn't easy. He had to be careful not to make a loud noise from his rings knocking on the marble walls.

The lights that Leopold thought were for helping them find their way in the dark became very different inside the temple. The walls and the columns looked like they were desperate sunbathers soaking in the light, then giving off a surreal, wavering glow. The boys stood on opposite sides of the cella, the inner chamber.

115

The old men continued with the girl, deep into the temple. Leopold moved along with them high in the corner where the wall met the ceiling, but he lost sight of them when they pushed her into a shrouded area, a small sunken room. He took a chance, moved closer, and lowered himself behind a large sculpture. He peeked over its shoulder. There was a high seat with three legs that she was being forced on top of, just like the seat she described. She grumbled and complained. Leopold couldn't hear her clearly but could make out a tone of doubt and hesitation. He saw the navel she spoke of. It looked like a giant large egg wrapped in a rope made of seashells. On either side were glittering gold eagles, their wings stretched out as if to embrace the whole world. Underneath her was a thin opening in the floor, like a crack, a faultline.

The priests moved closer, blocking Leopold's view of her.

He heard her voice more clearly; she was complaining that what she was doing was against Apollo, that it was not the ritual she was trained for. Leopold heard a loud slap. He saw them struggling and her arms flailing. She started to scream. Leopold was paralyzed with conflicting emotions. He imagined himself lunging at the men, tearing them away from her. He shouted "stop" and "get off of her," but couldn't tell if he even made a sound. No one heeded him. The light-bearers continued holding their trays, their heads down. The men began tearing the girl's clothing. Leopold was shaking. He'd never fought before, he wasn't quite sure how to do it, his strength was too dangerous. He was so angry, he felt he would kill them. He agonized as she screamed. He closed his eyes, lifted above the statue, and prepared to pounce.

21 – THE FIRST ANT

Convincing the commercial storage building to sell was easy, but bribing the thousands of customers to move all their mostly forgotten belongings to another storage property was a whole thing. Brink wanted this location for her first school, even though the building required millions of dollars in additional earthquake retrofitting and fire protection to keep her project safe. She saw it as the future hub of a new Los Angeles.

Day one of the Academy of NeuroTechnology included a series of interviews with *volunteers* gathered by the most monied individuals the world's ever known. Even Brink's ludicrously deep pockets were minuscule by comparison.

Brink was a little surprised to feel what she did when she met the first in line, not because he was famously the first man chosen to rocket to Mars, but because he was disarmingly handsome. She had been with more partners than usual since losing Shelby and never felt the heart tug once. She wasn't sure what was going on here, but she felt something. And it felt great.

She invited him to change into suitable garb for a medical clean room and then she and her trusty assistant, Sulis, ran him through a series of measuring tests. Nothing like the rigorous astronaut training stuff. More like a very invasive fitting for a suit one wears on the inside.

The tests were a little tedious, as was the Mars boy, Glas, and Brink found herself in her head, going over the ANT plan:

A world class educational research facility where she'd gather the world's sharpest science kids (Pittsburgh Pirates style, stolen from all the best schools, a little nod to her second home and alma mater). She'd get them working on cutting edge tech, medical research, and the new concern Brink liked to call Spacebrain™ (what space and other altered planetary atmospheres do to the human brain).

Brink's thinking drifted to her mother's work and her own origins in that context, especially since the primary purpose of this first ANT was so weirdly similar to what Semele ended up doing with her research grant as a postdoc. Brink's mother's infamous work on the biological basis of consciousness, a phenomenon Semele was convinced was yet another scam by evolution to trick an ape into the superpowered delusions of *free will* and *selfhood,* led directly to the birth of her first and only daughter. Semele was no heathen when it came to consciousness, free will, and selfhood; she knew those mechanisms were necessary, driving delusions, and her own delusion told her science wants no stone unturned.

The funders had no interest in the biology, the epistemology, the ontology, or the science really. They wanted to know whether identity was a mathematical and physical substrate that was extractable and, given the right conditions to maintain it, immortal.

Semele wasn't a sci-fi fan, even though she was pretty sure she could get close to what these oligarchs were after, but the funding allowed her to go full steam ahead with her crazy idea of manifesting what eggheads of the world would consider consciousness in a non-human primate.

And she did; Brink was born that year, March 7th, 2034.

And like Mother like daughter, Brink's Academy went through the motions for the wealthy while planning her own proof of consciousness. The Los Angeles ANT was an accredited graduate program second, and an incubator first. Brink and Shelby wanted a child. And so she would build one.

22 – WELCOME TO THE CENTER OF THE EARTH

Her scream stopped and was immediately followed by a groaning rumble. The building shook. Leopold opened his eyes and noticed the crack running under the girl's seat widen and splinter. The rumbling was a growl, becoming more throaty and viscous. The old men turned to run. One was held back, something wrapped around his leg. The others were howling in fear, scrambling for the exit. There was no longer a girl perched atop the tripod. She was covered in a writhing collection of limbs and scales growing at a mad pace, forming a serpentine shape. Its tail grew too large to hold the priest's leg, the control of its body undulating from one end to the other. The opening in the ground became a chasm, and the monster slipped into the hole, catching the edge with its snaking body and vestigial hands. It hung there, continuing to grow. As the opening started to tear at the walls of the temple, the creature rose, completing its transformation. It pulled its front legs out of the earth, a newborn, gangling dragon with wings spanning the temple's entire width. Its struggled flapping tore at the roof, pulverizing limestone. It threw itself out of the hole onto its long belly. Its arms crashed into the ground to steady itself. It opened its mouth and let out an execrable mesh of viscera, a white and yellow spray of unrecognizable foulness, covering the entirety of the temple, slamming the priests against the doors and sweeping the altar boys with its flood. The dragon's jaw opened further, a clicking sound rose up from its throat and a thick orange arc of flame blasted from its mouth, catching the thick substance, turning the inside of the temple into a roiling green inferno.

Leopold escaped through an opening in the collapsing roof. He circled above the temple as it buckled, falling in on the beast. Delphi was still quaking, columns twisting and falling everywhere. Leopold could see a dozen or so people evacuating buildings by the dancing red light of the temple conflagration. He flew over them all, as he searched desperately for Brink.

She was racing towards the temple, towards burning rock and the growing chasm.

The dragon was pushing through the debris of the demolished temple, emerging into the cool night, the embers of the burning stone skittering off its wings. Brink cocked her head. Her mouth fell open. It took a moment for her to register Leopold's shouting as he came swooping down to gather her.

She grabbed hold of his lower ring and Leopold launched them into the thermal air.

The monster noticed the enticing gliding pair, as if they were a large, tasty insect. A single flap of its wings pushed hurricane winds towards them as they tried to escape, but before Leopold could get halfway across the temple grounds, the creature was in front of them. It opened its mouth. Leopold turned, screaming at Brink to hold as tight as she could, and sprang off in the other direction. The foul gunk sprayed from the dragon's mouth, as if it were vomiting disease from its innards. It covered the entirely of Delphi. Brink saw the dragon draw its twisting neck back, sparks forming in its throat. When the flames began to form, she knew they wouldn't have time to get away.

"Go down," she shouted up at Leopold.

He heard her but couldn't believe she meant it and continued on.

She pointed emphatically at the black canyon growing ever longer and wider, devouring the remains of the temple and surrounding buildings. He didn't understand. The flames were coming, everything was igniting, melting, almost screaming as it raced to engulf them.

Brink let go.

Leopold felt her fall away, her limp body disappearing into the abyss. He extended his rings faster then he ever had and dropped into the darkness just as the flames scorched everything above.

He could see her beneath him by the light of burning rocks. He fought his way down dodging earth and sediment while he could still see. Or before she hit bottom.

It was too late. When Leopold caught up and grabbed hold of her, his abilities were compromised, and they tumbled together, down and down, the embers extinguishing until all was darkness. But they didn't stop. They simply slowed down, tumbling head over feet and rings. It wasn't from any kind of updraft. Moments later, not enough time to converse, but long enough to feel changing momentum, they settled on a surface. They were engulfed in black, nauseous and cold.

23 – THE UNBEARABLE WEIRDNESS OF INDIVIDUALITY

When Leopold was born, no one noticed. Not even his mother.

Midwives of a kind were present, but it just didn't register the way it should have. There was no goo to clean off, no cord to cut, no bottom to spank, and most disturbingly absent, no cry.

The original plan for the child, beyond his brain, included the software equivalent of a voice box and a stereo set of ears. As far as senses, that was it. At least that's what the first line designers knew. With those, it was expected he would learn language and eventually express himself, but there was nothing coming out and only a few asthmatic wheezes and general white noise going in. Sixteen researchers waited to see life emerge from a metallic console as if they were trying to deliver him themselves through their straining, furrowed brows. The image would have haunted Leopold for life, had someone been thoughtful enough to give him eyes from the start.

The readouts told them that they had succeeded, he had brain patterns identical to a very specific newborn, but they couldn't tell whether any more than a thing in a coma entered the world. The brain looked like it was still in a uterus of a kind - like a glowing abalone shell. His lobes were uniquely arranged. It wasn't necessary to follow the exact shape called for by his DNA, so the team, mostly his mom, streamlined his "processing".

Imagine starting life blind and paralyzed. All you have are variations in sound. Context would be the way the same sounds varied, and even then without interaction, those sounds would enable you to do nothing more than repeat them, if that. This was the universe Leopold lived in for the first day of his life, not black, not white, just a murmuring nothingness.

At exactly 12:06 in the afternoon of the next day, Jello Green fell off his stool. He never graduated high school, but he ran one of the most sophisticated laboratories in the world. He'd been watching and listening to Leopold for almost eight hours when he took a short break to check one more time whether a girl he met two nights ago at bowling, which he attended as a spectator, had sent him a message. That entire stretch, the only sound coming out of the "Leopold speaker" was a calm, steady tone, a translation of Leopold's brainwaves into an auditory signal so that Jello wouldn't have to look at a screen endlessly. Jello called it the "sound of aliveness." (To this day, if you visit the lab, which is now dedicated to some entirely different and far less interesting project concerning lampreys, and you get in any elevator, you'll hear the sound of aliveness spill out from the speakers, with a subtle backbeat and a plaque on the wall made to look like a screen, which reads: Current track - "The Sound of Aliveness" by Leopold and Jello Green.)

Jello had heard something strange. He wished it was a colleague who had snuck up on him, or a stray noise from the computer. Or worse, if it was only him, he feared he'd been witness to something too important for someone like him, that his affliction, which had served him so well in his job, had finally come to ruin it.

When he was just becoming old enough to notice girls, in addition to the flood of hormones that change the colors and smells of the world, like the acquisition of mutant powers gone terribly wrong, he was struck with a strange affliction called apraxia. Many odd brain disorders had been untangled over the last couple decades, but this one still eluded the best neurologists in the business, including Brink. The condition is a form of disconnection from learned motor activities. For example, if you were to say to Jello, "clean up your room," he could. If you were to say to him, "tuck the bed sheet in," he couldn't. He would most likely wave his hands over the bed, or push the bed, or maybe just stand there. But the first command, clean your room, led to something special in Jello, uncharacteristic of those with this disorder and certainly that of a regular teenager. Instead of hearing him moan and complain, you'd instead get the cleanest house in the neighborhood, perhaps then the cleanest neighborhood, including architectural plans for improving the home, streets, infrastructure, and if he wasn't too tired, a ten-year plan for residential resource allocation. That's what this lab had become for him, something he wasn't told to do, but something he already was, like an organic extension of those flailing limbs that worked perfectly fine.

He went to get others, to physically grab someone and drag them back to share what he'd heard, but before he got to the door, it was thrown open by one, then another scientist. It stayed open until people were lining up in the hallway to get close enough to hear the recording, like nervous parents desperately waiting to hear whether they've been given a healthy child. They'd all been listening remotely. The sound of aliveness:

mnnmnmnmnnmnmnnmn

There was an immediate, cooperative silence. The sound was unchanged:

nmnmnmnmnnmnnnmnmnnmmnmn

Someone went to replay the recording, but was slapped across the back by Jello, who was just trying to grab his arm. This was Jello's room and these were his controls. He sat down and cued up the aberration. 12:05:50. Jello hit play. The longest seconds ever recorded filled the room:

mmnmmn nmnmnnmmmn mnmnmnmnmnnmn

Then, after a slight increase in volume,

mmmnNMMI INNINIIII EEEEMMNM INM

the sounds became familiar:

IMM MM IMMM I M I M

As in i m i m as in "I am I am." As in, what on earth just happened? Then back to the beautiful drone of two consonants stretching into infinity:

I M I M M m mmnnmnnn mnnmmmm

Until Jello hit stop.

"Play it again!" cried at least four of those in attendance. The room was a cauldron of excited confusion. Brainwaves, themselves, do not speak. The phenomenon was kind of like resting one's head on someone's chest to listen to a heartbeat and suddenly hearing the heart say "I love you." Jello explained that the brainwave pattern was not the source of the speech, that the voice box had been activated, but how and why were beyond explanation.

For his own good, but also as most who worked on the project will still admit, to help them collect data, Leopold needed more actual inputs and outputs if he were going to make any sense to himself or others in the world. There was debate over whether to give him meta-human senses, which would have been very exciting but potentially disastrous. They had already beat very high odds birthing him in the first place and the previous project had already lost too many subjects to ambitious additions. Anyway, Leopold had a perfect emulation of a specific human brain, so it would have been ridiculous and unpredictably dangerous to start adding extra-human parts now. Everyone agreed to start small. Plus it wasn't their child, exactly. There were deeply trusted guides on this journey, but the boy was the love child of two already extraordinary people and the mother would not take kindly to messing about with an already almost miraculous birth.

The team got back to work to solve the first of a thousand expected hurdles to "consciousness" —

Stage One. Build Leopold Some Eyes.

The original project goal — "life" from a human genetic blueprint, was met. A child was born of the sexual combination of two individuals. A child, meaning an infant brain made out of a synthetic neural matrix designed to "grow" in an analogous way the biological version does. The rest of the genetic instructions were significantly "directed." He was not a robot. Not an A.I. A newborn grown from smart plastic instead of flesh.

How he would interface with the world was now up to a curious collection of bewildered caregivers.

By late morning of the second day, there were four designs floating around. Two of them were goggle-like attack-of-the-robot-slave shapes that would sit alone on a surface staring out at nothing in particular. One was an array of six eyes, all very small, the designer figuring Leopold would be a multitasker. The final design was nothing original, it was the latest in eye replacement technology, essentially exactly what goes with a bioplastic brain — bioplastic eyes. It was a great privilege that budget was never one of the hurdles.

The eyes worked. When they were hooked to Leopold, the visual regions of his brain exploded and the eyes lolled around just like a half-asleep, quarter-conscious baby's eyes. They sat on the console in front of the aquarium-like container that held his brain.

Jello spent the night watching his eyes. Leopold woke occasionally, the eyes bobbled about as if searching for Jello, then after finding him, went peacefully back to sleep. Though he knew turning his head slightly to watch the brain monitors would tell him all he needed to know, Jello became very worried when the eyes stayed closed. Was Leopold still asleep? Had we lost him? Should I have built him lungs I could watch expand and contract, he thought? He cycled though the distressing thoughts for hours. He didn't sleep at all that night. Instead, he sang. He leaned over, eyes heavy, resting his chin in his hands and sang groggily, the only songs he knew more than the choruses of, Beatles tunes. Leopold dreamed hopeful baby dreams. He really did.

The next morning, the lab was buzzing with new energy. Jello had become the default Project Head of the new stage of Operation Leopold, which meant that all new design ideas were plopped down on his desk and then eagerly discussed and argued over with the person who had plopped the previous one and the person plopping the next. They were mostly modifications or elaborations on sight and sound devices to help Leopold gather data faster and more efficiently, none of them exactly education-minded, just processing-speed-obsessed. Jello enjoyed the atmosphere and he thought Leopold did too, though he rejected all the ideas for the first week, and halfway through the next, until the strange sounds happened again.

It was just like one of those movies where the recently arrived human-looking alien tries to speak, struggles with the first few syllables of its first few words, then masters English within a couple sentences. It wasn't just like that, but it felt like it. During a heated design debate over retractable focal lenses, Leopold said:

Maaa k. Maaa kuh ma. maakm maaakme. Make me.

Jello and the three other people in the room knew this couldn't possibly mean what it sounded like, knew that Leopold must have heard those words a thousand times with all the discussions going on in there, but it was nonetheless inspiring.

One of the scientists in the room was Mina Mount.

On her way home that night, she began to cry. She was a wispy young woman with unfortunate glasses and flat, bobbed hair. She built interfaces before joining the team and was central to creating Jello's instrument display. She lived alone in a small apartment with a stuffed animal within reach anywhere you stood. She collapsed on her bed and continued to cry, nothing heavy, no sobs, but unstoppable. She rolled over and made a call.

"What's happened? What's wrong?"

"Nothing, mom."

"Were you fired?"

"God. No. Don't start."

"Well, tell me. This is what happens when you live so far from home."

"I get yelled at?"

"I'm not yelling. I haven't heard you crying like that since that boy turned gay on you."

"He didn't *turn* … hargh, just nothing. Nothing is wrong." Mina started laughing. A cathartic laugh, her final tears falling from her cheeks onto her most precious furry creature, e. e. oof. She picked up e. e. oof, which looked kind of like a dog, but mostly like a towel-upholstered sugar cookie that wanted to be a dog, and stared. E. e. oof's ear shape was completely sucked away, the texture almost like micro-fiber from the endless grips of love.

"Is there another boy?"

Mina got up from the bed excitedly, gripping e. e. oof and smiling. She threw her coat back on, shoved the doll in her pocket, and ran out the door, her mother's warning voice trailing behind.

"You know why your father left us!"

Mina got back to the lab quickly, her pulse elevated, her eyes crisp and bright with a twinkle that comes only after a long cry turns out to be inspired joy. Jello was in the middle of the na na nas of Hey Jude when she approached the door. Before this night, she had been intimidated by Jello, but now she felt stronger than any man. She felt like a wave.

She took a couple of breaths, pushed the door open, and announced, "We need to chew his ears off!"

Jello stopped singing, embarrassed. "Dr. Mount. I didn't see you there."

"I think we need to pull him out of there. I think he needs touch. Touch first. Touch before sight or hearing or x-ray vision or megaphone voice. Leopold's a baby. He needs love!"

Jello, to his surprise, had pulled up a chair for Mina to join him the moment she came in the room. He gestured to it the best he could and said, "What do you have in mind?"

Stage One. Build Leopold Some Eyes.
Stage One. Build Leopold Some Arms.

"This is where I helicopter in, gang," said Brink to a shocked and delighted crew of the best

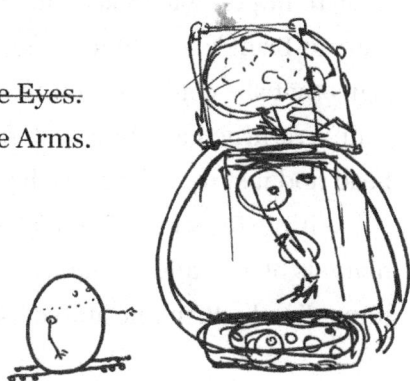

131

and brightest of Brink's Academy of Neurotechnology, or ANT as she was thrilled to call it, this Los Angeles location being the first of many global iterations.

"It is never a question of trust when I show up," she said, "It's either me being jealous, insistent, or dare I say it, full motherly."

"It is always a thrill when you grace us with your magic presence, milady," Jello said, sincerely, "I was gonna say you missed some big moments, but I'm sure you didn't."

Brink winked and smiled.

"If you're already moving to a chassis, I wanna supervise the use of the SCkin™. I've made some tweaks."

One of the ways Leopold's design was analogous to a bog standard human was instead of cells burning glucose for energy, his body, no matter which age-appropriate size, was covered with a fancy, easily altered polymer, a solar cellular source of energy — his SCkin, cooked up by dad with mom adding just the right seasoning.

No one was surprised and everyone was relieved when Brink opened the large box she brought with her, revealing a rather realistic looking baby body. She'd calculated that he was already approaching a year, cognitively, so had the prothesis master designer build for that. That designer was Mina, who found it close to impossible to keep her shadow work a secret from the team at Brink's insistence. She stared hard at Brink, looking for signs that she could burst into screams of joy and pride. Brink of course returned an equivocal, flirty, nose-scrunching smirk with a head nod just to make sure she'd need to use the restroom soon.

With Brink's help, it took less than ten hours to pair the marvels of love and technology. Leopold's arms grasped immediately. Brink hesitated. She'd never been more in love, but she felt, in the middle of her, that the first to hold this boy should be Mina or Jello, or ideally both.

As everyone waited for the moment, Brink leaned into the crib Mina had made, lifted tiny Leopold, and held him out for Mina to hold. Mina fell apart, inconsolably crying. Brink laughed, loudly, the way only a new mother is allowed to laugh at pain. She shifted her pose towards Jello, carefully cupped Leopold in her right arm, and extended her left towards Mina as she drew Jello over with her eyes. Jello shook his head.

"We'll do it together. Mina, get over here. Jello. Trust me." Brink said.

She'd already held her boy. Mina told herself that was witnessed and logged, and she was clearly dying to do it herself. Brink handed him carefully to Jello and draped her long arm around his shoulders and brought Mina to help support Leopold from below. She stepped away and Jello, looking as calm as he could, stared into Mina's eyes with emotion he'd never felt. Mina smiled harder than she knew she could and Brink, to her amazement, teared up. It had been awhile.

"Later kids, call me when he's done with diapers," Brink said as she left the room.

Earnest laughter from those still around, and true paranoia from Jello, who gave Leopold's full weight to Mina. Could've been any weight. Mina had him.

Jello and Dr. Mount worked very late, reviewing some troubling delta wave patterns. It appeared that Leopold was dreaming then fading out then returning to dreaming, meaning it looked like he would dream a little, then die a little, then come back to the same dream. It wasn't exactly time to panic – the "fade out" was nothing like the previous experiment's failure –

but any abnormality was not a good sign. They did not call Brink yet. They called in the superstar brain wave members of the team, who were not happy to be woken from their own dreams. It would take an hour or so for them to arrive, so Jello and Mina stood quietly over the crib. They looked down at a pair of cold, tucked arms, disturbingly rapid eyes in REM, and possibly dying bioplastic brain visible through the transparent but otherwise anatomically realistic head. It didn't matter. He was beautiful. Leopold was their whole world now. They reached out instinctively to caress his hands, smiling at one another for having the same idea at the same time. Leopold reached out with both of his arms to hold their fingers and squeeze the best he could. A charged air filled the room. Jello and Mina's eyes grew wide, and tears filled their eyes. Mina made that sound that's half-cry and half-laugh, as if the world had just been saved from the brink of disaster. Jello wanted desperately to take Mina's hand, but knew he would end up punching her in the face or something equally frustrating. She took his.

They were married six months later.

The memory of that wedding are catastrophically mythic now. The ceremony was simple, beautiful. Mina, who had already been working on it, had, over those six months, taught Jello's mind to calm enough to allow his mind to repair with the help of Brink's connector therapy, a strange boon of the IMAC.

Mina and Jello obsessively preserved the memory of that time because during the reception, just days after Leopold had prematurely begun marching around, Brink dove to lift him then push the newly married couple and anyone else in the path through the mid-level atrium out to the terrace just as the ground began to shake. It was no usual tremor. And in a building Brink spend hundreds of millions on retrofitting, the unusually slow rocking still obviously indicated a bad earthquake. The Sierra Madre-Cucamonga fault lines had triggered a cascading rupture, setting off a vast system of faults across the LA Basin. From that terrace, as fear replaced every other feeling the day brought, those who were still on their feet watched in disbelief as the entirety of Los Angeles County erupted in flames, almost simultaneously.

Brink shouted for everyone to move back into the building, assuring and forceful.

"This building is going nowhere. We have to be inside for the fire suppression to kick on!"

They trusted their leader and just as everyone was past the threshold, the glass dome normally over the outer atrium came down and the building became deluged with a thick foam.

Evacuation was disastrous and the County lost millions of lives. Millions more left never to return. There was nothing to return to initially.

Eventually the evacuation was complete with the surrounding states and Northern California doing an incredible job with the refugees, a skill they tragically acquired from the Water Wars.

Brink had spent all of her time since opening the school carefully studying what she resisted calling the zeitgeist of Southern California with her early use of the IMAC tied directly to the Ghat network. Because of her special brand of procrastination, she'd developed a comprehensive plan for how to make Los Angeles a sustainable and dependable region.

After the fires were finally extinguished, there was a call to meet in Sacramento for a future of L.A. meeting. The Governor invited Brink. They both had a plan that turned out to be quite similar.

The first session wrapped early as the elected and representative figures in attendance were too busy dealing with the now. Brink and the Governor had a private moment and both spoke at the same time:

"You need to come out," said the Governor.

"I need to step up," said Brink.

"We saying the same thing?" asked the Governor.

"Probably. I need to direct TWF efforts. That it?"

"Exactly that. You okay with this?"

"Doesn't matter. Shelter comms?

The Governor nodded.

The announcement spread as fast as both had hoped. The world's only transgenic person, uniquely telegenic and incomparably charismatic, was now astride culture as few have been in history. Brink put out a call for a careful collection of TWF leaders to prepare for a major operation: The Los Angeles RECEP. This introduced her term for reconceptualizing major metropolitan centers as sustainable, quilted communities, dedicated to post-scarcity, positive, healthy living.

It took weeks to even carve work roads into the devastation, accomplished only thanks to the cooperative efforts of well paid corporate entities, the armed forces, and legions of TWF members from around the globe.

The ANT had indeed survived the catastrophe and it had its own power sources, but its focus transformed completely into the primary TWF headquarters. The scientists and students who stayed joined the RECEP. The others transferred easily to international schools, but Brink's first priority was a difficult conversation for her and she imagined for the newlyweds. She begged them to immediately engage their role as Leopold's godparents and take him to another city for an indeterminant number of years. Brink pitched Pittsburgh, the world's robotics capital and home to many of her friends and old classmates, several who could help with Leopold's unique needs.

Jello and Mina jumped at the opportunity, barely registering the reason Brink gave — to protect him from all those still vehemently opposed to the TWF. They picked Vancouver, Mina being half-Canadian. Brink bought them a lovely home and remotely began construction on her future home in the mountains above Squamish.

Mina's account of Leopold's youth was as sacrosanct as it was unreliable. Brink could never bring herself to ask Leopold to clarify anything as the memory of his step-mom was too precious.

The story as Brink knew it was that Leopold was progressing nicely in school. He was near the top of his class and agreed to skip a grade, though he stayed in touch with his friends while he made new ones. He was eight and it had been a couple years since he was given a new body. When Robbie Bentley moved to the area and arrived at school, he asked Leopold to carry his books for him. Leopold obliged for the entire day since they coincidentally had the same teachers. At the end of the day, Robbie carefully articulated his home address hoping his new robot assistant would come over to play games with him. Robbie was a little spoiled and assumed his parents had sent him this cool gift to make up for making him move away from his friends. Leopold picked up on Robbie's misunderstanding about three seconds after he made the mistake, but was so tickled by the surreality of the situation, he played along. Mina was there after school to pick him up, but Leopold motioned that he'd be going with Robbie, following a few steps behind him and forcing a funny robot walk to project to his mom what was happening. Mina didn't get it, but did understand the "I'm going to a friend's house" look. Mina and Jello never let Leopold travel too far alone for fear of kidnapping, whether mistaken as an expensive robot or by those who knew what a unique entity he was. And especially who he was related to. Mina waved approval. Then she got on her bike and followed at a safe distance. When she realized that she didn't recognize Robbie as the boys approached his front door, Mina raced into Robbie's yard and skid to a stop. Robbie was startled. Leopold stifled a laugh. Mina leapt off the bicycle and the skid and crash flushed Robbie's mom from inside the house. Leopold burst out in an embarrassed, guilty laugh.

"Mom. Easy. I'm sorry. This is my fault. I should have known you'd follow us," he continued as he embraced her. Robbie's mom arrived mystified. Robbie could not have looked any more perplexed.

"Mom?" cried Robbie, no one knowing whether he was repeating Leopold or calling to his own mom.

"What is going on out here?" Robbie's mother, Faith, asked with a neighborly smile and an eyebrow raised.

"I really do have to apologize," said Leopold to a Robbie who looked about to cry. "I was just messing with you and I have to admit I had no idea how far I was going to take it." Faith's face lit up with excitement. "Oh my goodness! Is that Leopold?" It may have been something with the family, no one knew who she addressed that question to, if it was a question. Mina finally pieced it together, the robot gesture now making sense and making her stifle a snort. She approached Faith, who was holding Robbie's shoulders.

"I'm Mina and this is my son, Leopold. Very nice to meet you, Robbie." She exchanged a knowing look with Faith, who also understood her son had paid a price for his presumption.

"The robot kid?" blurted Robbie. "I mean the kid who ... I mean, you're a kid?"

Leopold helped him out. "I'm the robot kid, yeah. Only I write my own program." With that, Leopold blinked which even to him was a very disturbing image. He thought it a perfect last touch to the ruse.

Robbie and Leopold became best friends. Mina even eased up on the surveillance since Robbie lived so close to school and Faith was there. She ran a small business from home and her husband was a surgeon. Robbie was also an only child and from that point on, he was less spoiled. But only a little less.

Life was going well for Leopold.

And then he noticed he was attracted to some of his peers, boys and girls. He was less confused about the pansexuality than he was about how hormones worked for him. He might have been the first kid who initiated *that* chat with his parents.

Leopold's eye was mostly on someone in class Leopold had known for several years. They spent very little time talking or hanging out. She had been at his sixth birthday party, but at that point she registered as little more than the person who was lame at group chess. Now she was something else. Leopold was well versed in sexuality on its surface since young people had access to any and all information on the topic. But this was different. How different was due to early decisions made in the scope of Leopold's brain design.

There are parts of all vertebrate brains that create hormones that create more hormones for use in stimulating certain body functions. When Mina introduced more realistic and technologically elaborate bodies for Leopold, she also asked a very important question – is Leopold a man or a snail? Leopold had a sense of smell and a full range of emotions, though an enormous amount of money had to be spent to get all that right, or what everyone hoped was right. They strictly followed his genetic code, as they had for his brain, which spelled out, among other things, low-to-average testosterone-leveled heteroflexible male. They had built the feedback systems that define what goes with that sexual identity in his early youth, but now puberty was in their face, and there was a little problem.

Leopold sat on the couch with Randi Bloom at five o'clock in the evening. The details of their time together are private of course, though one mortifying fact was exposed at the end of the week in class. Leopold was chatting with another girl, a girl everyone knew to be "experienced" with boys. This girl, who will remain nameless, turned her head toward Randi and made a naughty gesture with her hand and mouth. She then turned her head back to Leopold and put her hand on his lower back. The girl was incensed and, in a well-meaning gesture meant to protect her man, instead hung him out by screaming at the girl, "He doesn't even have a penis, you slut!" Randi slapped her hands over her mouth.

It was probably the case that if anyone stopped to think about it, they would have wondered whether he did have one, but no one had ever stopped to think about it, surprisingly. Now it was the only thing anyone could think about. Leopold didn't help matters by storming out of the classroom. It turned out to be the least of his worries that day.

With horrible irony, his mom was at that moment procuring said appendage from a laboratory across town. After the date with Randi, she and the team had decided that his next body, if not the current one, be outfitted with the conspicuously absent member. It was a ludicrously conservative, though unintentional, omission.

Even as a scientist, she blushed when picking up the accessory from a giggling roboticist. Afterward, she went to sit with Robbie at Leopold's afterschool football game. Robbie didn't take to football. He was uncoordinated and the ball never seemed to behave at his feet, but he eagerly supported the team and his buddy.

Her plan was to walk home with Leopold, give the package to Jello and let him bequeath the gift unto his son then or later that night. She had a number of hearty, embarrassed private laughs about whether she should wrap it with a ribbon. She considered going out for the evening, knowing Jello would make her present it herself.

When Mina arrived, Leopold wasn't at the game. Robbie was there, waiting, and told her he hadn't seen him since an earlier class. Mina approached a girl she recognized and asked if she'd seen Leopold. The girl explained the penis incident from lunch and how much it upset him. Mina felt awful and hoped Leopold had just wandered home or to the model shop he enjoyed a few blocks away. She called the house, but there was no answer. She called Jello at work who said he hadn't seen him and asked if he should worry. She said, "No. No, I'm just nervous about his new … you know, thing. Love you." Those were the last words Jello heard from his wife.

Along a shortcut to the model shop, where Leopold sat melancholy for the first time ever, Mina walked mindlessly across the street. She was hit by an old, silent electric service vehicle.

Jello and Leopold were by her side in the hospital day and night, when allowed. She was on life support. After a few days, Jello made a fateful decision. Her brain had suffered serious damage and more than most people, he knew she wasn't going to survive long and during that time, she wouldn't have an identity she or anyone else could understand. Her brain was barely able to keep her alive with the machines attached to her. He signed the paperwork. Her life support was removed. He felt angry at her. It felt like she'd possessed him to do the job. He thought maybe she did that to give him strength to carry on.

The tragedy brought Jello closer to his son, but it was short-lived. A week after her funeral, Jello explained what Mina was up to the day she was lost and tried to give him the gift. He assumed it would be in the spirit of renewal, a positive look towards the future. Leopold heard it as only one thing. He was responsible for her death.

Jello was always an excellent father, but his neurological disorder made it impossible for him to be a primary caregiver. The consultants were still there, and Brink did what she could from a distance, but Leopold was mostly self-sufficient by then. He became dark and introverted after the accident. He spent all his time with study, obsessing over eugenics and replacing parts of himself, never quite attempting what would be the equivalent of suicide for him, but certainly analogous to self-mutilation. He quit sports. He almost quit school. Robbie and his family moved away. It was never made explicit, but his parents couldn't handle the effect Leopold's gloom and the strange and unpredictable nature of Jello's household had on their son.

By the time Leopold started his senior year of high school, he had alienated almost everyone he knew, including instructors. Though his grades had slipped, he was still going to graduate and the independent work his did, mainly on his own body, had the best universities in the world clambering to accept him, all with free rides.

That first day of his last school year was something the other students and faculty will never forget. It was the first time they saw his new look.

He had removed his fake skin. He wore no clothes. Though odd, those were things they would expect of him. What struck everyone with a mixture of pity, disgust, and existential distress was that Leopold had removed his legs. His new design incorporated his own modification of a technology used mainly in space and with industrial robots. He moved around on three undulating diamagnetic rings beginning at his waist and holding him off the ground so that he essentially stood eight feet tall. No one said a word about it. Except for one kid. Between classes, Leopold tried to float past a kid in a fruitleather jacket. The kid wouldn't let him by.

"Why are you here?"

"Get out of my way, please."

"Make me, junkpile."

Leopold stared down. It was a girl, wide shouldered, with terrible hair. She reminded him of his mother. "I'm not in the mood for this," he moaned.

"What are you made of? I wanna know."

Leopold felt nervous. He couldn't understand it. He had the power to move her out of the way in any number of ways, but something about her defiance, her confidence, made Leopold hesitate and almost cower. He liked the feeling. Twenty seconds before, he felt nothing at all. He started to laugh. It was a strange sight, like a ghost stopping to have a laugh at the living and in doing so, coming back to life.

"I will mess you up. Stop laughing," she said nervously.

Leopold lowered himself, so he looked directly into her eyes.

"You don't freak me out."

"I don't?" Now Leopold felt anxious. He felt a confused rage building up inside him. He couldn't understand this kid at all. "I don't freak you out? What is wrong with you?"

"Nothing. You're the one who thinks something's wrong with them." Who the hell was this kid, thought Leopold. A crowd had formed around them, including fascinated adults.

"Wait a minute, are you new here?"

She didn't answer.

"Do you know I'm not a robot?"

"Say what?"

"What do you think I am?"

"You're like a security guard or something?"

Leopold burst out laughing. "What, did you think you were some tough chick standing up to the school vacuum cleaner?"

"Haha. Yeah, sort of. What the heck are you?"

Leopold moved back a little and retracted his rings as two black metal legs extended from within his torso. He stood on solid ground and put his hand out.

"I'm a Green. Leopold Green. What are you?"

"I'm a Carson. Sulis Carson."

Brink has always adored this story. Leopold told her this one directly.

Los Angeles was shockingly populated by this point and Brink, having worried about Leopold the whole time, but especially since Mina's passing, spent every day reflecting on Jello's plea with Brink to spend more time with him. Leopold had been spending his summers at Brink's Canadian home, Prudence, since he was "twelve" but Brink knew that Jello's anguish made his already difficult job close to impossible. It was very lucky Leopold aged out of sync with your blood and guts kid and was able to take good care of himself.

Brink found herself crying some nights from the conflict between being an absent mother and a city builder. She had to get Los Angeles to a flow state and that was some years away. This led to a grand eureka for their relationship — Brink invited Leopold, who she noticed innovated diamagnetic levitation beyond anyone else's imagination with his ring system, to consult on the design and implementation of the network of levitrains the LA Basin required. A smashing success. Leopold loved being in the blooming L.A. and found himself eager to join the family business, which he thought was advanced urban design?

Jello called him every day of course, and Leopold sent endless photos, especially shots of Leopold helping build the Sun Tower Arrays, an elaborate coastal low-energy membrane-based desalinization plants. Leopold thought up multiple uses for the excess salt collected from sea bricks to industrial needs. The effluent actually enriched marine ecosystems and fog catchers helped supplement inland irrigation and humidity control.

There was no longer pollution in Los Angeles. No personal cars allowed (one of several reasons why many former residents gave up on returning).

Leopold's trains connected hubs throughout the city, in addition to connecting surrounding cities. The globally crucial L.A. port's move made San Diego a much richer city and utterly transformed Santa Barbara. Los Angeles was now the green gem between two ecological messes.

24 – I FORGOT MY HOT PANTS

"Do you feel a floor?" Brink said. "This is strange."

"This? This is strange?" Leopold launched into a chorus of expletives.

"Are we in hell?" he howled. "Have you taken us to a place I would never ever ever ever have believed in before but now have absolutely no idea whether there are forces beyond my understanding? Could it simply be the worst dream ever? Or have you really done it? Have you created a madness-inducing time machine that twists up reality and fantasy so that the future will never be the same and we're trapped in a pit in time limbo forever? What are we supposed to do now anyway? I can't even tell if I'm really here! I don't feel a thing. Are you there? Is that you laughing? What is happening?!" His rage-filled voice was giving way to tremulous fear.

It was hard for her to remember how young he was when he'd accomplished and survived so much already. She quickly reassured him, "I'm here. I feel a surface beneath us now. Come closer. Give me your hand. I'm trying to check on what's going on."

"You're trying? You can't?" Leopold said as his panic grew.

"Hi there," interrupted a new voice. Leopold let out a shriek. The voice was syrupy, but casual, feminine, but broad and deep.

Leopold spun around and fell to his knees. The ground was uneven and a little moist. He could smell it, slightly grassy, like wet moss.

"Who is that? Brink? Was that you?"

He was answered with the flicker of a light, barely a candle. A man stood before them with his hand up in a greeting. Brink stood in front of Leopold, her shape barely discernible. They were in what looked like a cave, a passage only wide enough for single-file movement.

"You are seeing him, right?" whispered Leopold.

Brink approached the man slowly.

"Please say something," Leopold pleaded to Brink.

It was difficult to process the man's appearance, even though he was the most well-lit object in the cramped space, as if the light were emanating from his pores, a slow trickling fount of luminosity. But even though it was radiance, the light was still somehow dark, as if the purpose of the faint illumination was to emphasize how dark it truly was around him.

Brink stood less then a yard from the man. Was he really that tall? Was his hair alive? Was he a woman, though his mostly bare chest was flat?

"If you're here, I suppose there must be a real mess up there?" he said to them both.

Brink looked back at Leopold and the expression on her face worried him more than anything else had on the trip. As far as he could tell in the darkness, she looked totally confused.

"We should get moving. There's a lot of ground to cover," the man said softly.

He started away, taking the light with him.

Leopold could feel his sense of physicality going too. He hurried to catch up with him, sliding past Brink, who seemed caught up in distracted contemplation.

Brink's loitering stopped the stranger.

"Come along, beautiful creature," he said, reaching out to her with his teasing long fingers.

She followed, still preoccupied.

The man's shoulders rose and fell in a way that made it look like he was hardly strolling, but the ground he covered was vast. They walked along what felt like a subtle declination, the man several paces ahead of them.

Leopold spoke over his shoulder, "You have no idea what's happening, do you?" His tone was respectful. He finally felt like they were both suffering.

"I have an idea, but it's not a great one."

"We're dead, aren't we?"

"That would be very interesting, but no. I think we're a little off map."

"A little off map?" he said pronouncing each word like a countdown to keep from blowing his top, as if their underworld guide, disturbed by a blown top, would run off and leave them to dissipate into nothingness.

"What did you mean you're checking?" he whispered. "Are you or are you not horrified and lost and convinced we are never going to see our friends or possessions ever again?"

"I realize this won't help much at this point, but I have to say it. Don't worry."

"Really?"

"Seriously. Don't worry."

She could see he wasn't satisfied with her content-free reassurance, but it kept him from losing it.

She thought a little more false hope might encourage a helpful discussion and said, "We're probably not in any danger."

"Probably?" he said shrilly, still in a whisper.

"I shouldn't have said probably. There is a high probability that everything is not completely out of our control."

"What makes you say that? Mom, please. If you know something, I'd really like in on it."

"The honest truth is I don't have the ability to check anything at the moment and I have no idea why," she said.

Though she hadn't really answered, it was the first glimmer of troubleshooting Leopold had seen and it calmed him.

"Let me try something," Brink said confidently, inspiring even more comfort in Leopold.

Brink squeezed past Leopold and caught up to their mysterious guide. The closer she got, the more inexplicably excited and overwhelmed she became, so that by the time she reached him, she was a quivering mess. It took enormous effort to summon a thought, let alone ask a question. "Hu... he. Uh. Excuse me? Back here. Big man. Hey."

The man twisted, his rippling, perfect shoulders brushing against the walls of the dark cavern. He bent to face her. She peed herself a little.

His hair was long, a black waterfall of waves and curls. The planes and lines of his face were dizzying traps leading to his deep, fervid eyes, his expression like a soothing song, his every movement a carnal attack. He was at least two or three feet taller, but didn't so much tower as envelop when he stood before her.

Brink had enjoyed the attention of some of the world's most beautiful, most rugged, most enigmatic and engaging men and woman on earth, but it was as if she were now with a man available to women exclusively in their most intimate dreams, who was not really a man so much as an invited force.

The "wh" sound of who was the most she could muster before she collapsed, her eyes betraying her with a flutter as she fainted into his arms.

Leopold wasn't sure what had happened. Brink was still his symbol of strength and protection, his leader, and now she'd been killed by an odd-looking giant.

"That was unexpected," the bewildered man said, his voice melodic and friendly. "She's not faking, is she?"

Leopold, unsettled by the man's casual manner and that he addressed him at all, nervously shrugged.

"I'll carry her, shall I?"

He lifted and cradled Brink, then moved on.

"She's okay?" Leopold asked.

"I presume so. Her chest moves and her mind is active."

They continued on, Leopold following a little closer now. "Could you, if you can, could you tell me where we're going?" he asked.

"There is only one person who can solve your problem, child."

"Problem? Are we talking about the same problem?"

"The python, Delphyne. My cousin's enemy has returned."

"Python? What are you saying?" Leopold was surprised at his bold tone, but something about the stranger's submissive nature made even Leopold feel manly.

151

"We're going to the land of perfect sun where my brother-cousin vacations in winter. Only he can defeat the monster that's been unleashed to destroy Man's world."

"Of course. You had to say something like that while Brink was asleep," Leopold said, resigned to the absurdity. He put his head down and dutifully marched on.

Leopold got lost in thought, mostly in memories of his school friends, especially Sami. He was reminded of the time they were desperate to see their own perfect southern Californian sun after adventuring underground along the circuitous network of metro tunnels for way too long one day. They felt like worms until they ran across people who lived down there. It was strange, but not scary. It took a lot to scare Sami, and Leopold was often too future-minded to worry about the predicaments they got into. The duo knew few normal boundaries.

By the time Leopold snapped out of his reminiscences, he wasn't sure how long they had traveled. It could have been minutes, hours. Time felt weird. And he was surprised to find his environment easier to discern. There was an increase in the ambient light, separate from that emitted by the man. Perhaps a light at the end of tunnel, he thought. The tunnel looked organic, slightly disgusting, its rocky insides now glistened a bit.

Brink's eyes opened.

Her body was warm and comfortable. "That was the best sleep I've had in years. I think I figured out who you were in that last lucid part." Staring up into his beautiful face, Brink said, "Dionysus, I presume?"

"I am at times called that."

"Wild," Brink cooed.

"We have almost arrived. Would you like me to put you down?"

"Never."

"Sweetie, your lovely boy made a mess. I hate to say this, since you look like that, but you'll want to clean it up... unless you want to party first?"

"Feeling better then?" Leopold grumbled from the rear.

"Much."

"Then how about an explanation?" he said, surprisingly calm. "Something has gone wrong with the simulation, hasn't it?"

"Not wrong exactly."

"And you can't wake us up because something's happened to your control."

"That part is true but only very recently," said Brink. "I seem to be being rescued so good news."

She reluctantly wriggled out of the god's embrace and stood on her own two feet which felt renewed and tingly. She turned back to Leopold. "Yes, something has gone wrong, but if we're still together and active, then there are only so many things that could have happened, and most of them are nothing to worry about."

"Rescued?! I feel so much better now," Leopold said.

"Oh good, because I think things are going to get a lot weirder."

"I think I might hate you."

The cave filled with a soft light. Their guide made a sharp left. When they reached the turn, a large opening was revealed, and blinding sunlight poured in.

Their eyes adjusted slowly, images forming as if they were seeing for the first time in their lives.

They were outside the cave on a cliff-hugging path. The god had paused but continued on when they emerged, his long legs moving along the narrow rut of a path like a tightrope walker.

Leopold followed after him, struggling to master the gravity here.

When Brink caught up with them at the top of the cliff, they stood again on the scorched ground of Delphi. Dionysus put out his hand. Brink cocked her head since she no longer needed help and wasn't used to someone flirting harder than her. Leopold stood entranced with a new figure standing in front of a vanquished giant dragon-snake-monster.

This new man shouted at Brink as if a commander on a battlefield, "The python was no effort for me to dispatch. The philosopher is your responsibility. And I don't even like that word. Good luck to you, strange woman."

"What a prick," thought Brink. "As expected." She laughed to herself, and worried for a sec that gods read minds maybe? If he did, he didn't care about the opinion of a sexy chimera. "What a waste, he's so hot in those sparkly tight shorts."

"OMG I totally love you," Brink heard a voice either say out loud to her or from another dimension. At this point, she was just letting it all happen.

"Not only can we read your minds, we are thrilled when those minds put my douchebag brother in his place. You are right, he is soooo boring. And yes, of course I can solve your transportation problem. You will end up dying doing it the way you were thinking."

"I am honored, milord? Look how cute you are oh my gawd, eh, so... uhhh ... holy shit, you're Hermes! Now we are talking! When can I see the outfit?"

154

"You ready to go?" asked Hermes.

"Leopold. Get over here! You're gonna love this."

Leopold was done. And his apparently hallucinating mother wasn't making things better. Before he'd made up his mind about whether to just walk away, he found his body betraying him. His rings had extended against his "will" and they were moving completely illogically, as if he were a doll being played with.

Hermes had torn open the air in front of the mother and son and sent Leopold through it. Brink, slightly disappointed to miss out on playing with the gods some more, leapt quickly through.

An old man stood stupefied in front of Leopold and Brink, who were just as stunned to see their old boating friend again.

25 – I NEED TEN MINUTES

The service bot hadn't been connected to the house for many years, though it still had full access, being Brink's favorite electric goofball. He'd been gifted to her as a house warming present soon after Prudence was completed by a colleague Brink worshipped — her chief RECEP architect, Masa. The robot's appearance was captured perfectly by the name Masa gave him: Monkeybot, a stout, abstract chimp tank, with a long tray arm and a carefully designed personality to drive Brink nuts.

"Has anyone heard the one about the monkey and her best friend? They were prime mates!" said Monkeybot into the Prudence PA system, addressing a few random workers and about forty moaning students. "Priority One, though, for reals, please alert Duana and Fenix. Report to Level 3 IMAC LABS. Brink is experiencing a bad day. I am investigating now."

Monkeybot rolled across the scuffed hardwood floor of a vast living room with stunning snow-capped mountain views toward the glass-walled IMAC stations. He noticed that Brink had been uncharacteristically unmoving for some time. He tapped the glass of the lab door, as if part of his vaudeville routine, knowing whether alert or not, Brink would never hear it. "Land shark," he mumbled.

Realizing he is playing to an empty room and an uninterested remote crowd, he opened the door and rolled next to Brink. He performed scans a little too complicated for him. He asked Prudence to help out, knowing how sensitive a machine the IMAC was. The home purred at Monkeybot, "This is serious. Please leave the room."

"I have never been more insulted. And I've been insulted by the best!" Monkeybot complied and rolled out the door, swiveled, and leaned his head on the glass.

"It's not like I'm not seeing exactly what you're seeing and I'm like, concerned about it. I swear."

"Please be quiet," Prudence asked.

"Brink! Wake up! I'm being judged harshly!"

Prudence had already cut Monkeybot from the IMAC network. Brink remained motionless. Prudence awaited commands from Sulis, Fenix, Glas, or a few members of the TWF who demanded to remain unknown.

Monkeybot was able to discern the signal that was intercepting the GHat feed and adeptly blocked it from its invasion of Brink's mind. Brink immediately sat up and shouted, "I need ten minutes!"

"DO NOT pull me out of the sim. And thank whoever woke me up. You get extra rations and if it's who I think it is, a forty minute set in the upper auditorium!"

"Mama, this is an unprecedented and serious breach, we must solve this right away," Prudence told Brink inside her sim ear.

"Holy shit, for a second I thought you said that so Monkeybot could hear it. Maybe calling me mama was as bad an idea as it sounded. Ma'am was driving me insane. What am I doing ... I gotta go. Don't sweat anything until I come back. Stand the fuck down, you beautiful house!"

26 – LOOK WHAT YOU DID, ARISTOCLES!

"Why don't you look more astounded to see us?" Brink asked, exhausted and worried about what was coming next.

"I have assumed that your amazing boy was successful in rescuing you and having successfully delivered the young girl to Athens, you are both checking up on me because I am the only Greek you know who is thrilled to make your acquaintance."

"I get why your career was so rewarding. That was damn quick," Brink said, putting her arm around Leopold and moving in for a hug.

Protagoras happily obliged and embraced them both.

"I really wish that is why we are here. I really do. I've missed you. And I wish I could take you with me to my world, where scholars are finally understanding the voice you always had."

"And now what the endless beans is going on?" Leopold asked Brink with an exhaustion she'd never heard from him before.

"My darling sweet boy, I realize that you really don't need to be here for this. I release you!"

"Weren't we here to get tickets for a fuckin play? When is that happening?"

"All in good time, theatre lover. For now, hang with Sulis and tell her dinner and drinks are on me."

"Damn right they are."

With that, Leopold's body collapsed.

"Once again, he's fine. Let me properly explain," Brink said to the old man, who looked as if he had perhaps wandered into a play himself.

"Remember how you could tell I was lying to you about myself and where I'm from."

"I could never forget that. There will never be another face like yours."

"Truer words!" Brink smiled, then shut her face down and concentrated.

"You and I are currently tricks, oh wait ... do you know Plato's cave thing ... no dammit of course not ... you're supposed to be dead or ya know 'exiled' way before he writes that shit.

"Okay, I'm just going to not confuse myself and explain what's happening. My Greek probably isn't up for this but here goes: I built a contrivance that lets people see things that have already happened. You and I are inside that instrument right now. More specifically, I am in it seeing you, who lived over 2000 years before my time. That's the first part."

"I can tell you are telling a truth, but I am not pleased that I believe you," Protagoras said, mouth agape. "Perhaps it is the fear in your voice that matches my own, for some reason. Why are you afraid?"

"I am afraid because of how my machine works and the effect you and my son have had on the people of my time."

Protagoras began walking, knowing Brink will continue and follow.

"In the future, your work is almost entirely lost. This is because Plato vilified most philosophers who came before Socrates, especially the sophists."

Protagoras nodded.

Brink shook her head in amazement and continued, "I am guessing that you must have been murdered on that boat ride, or at best, anything you wrote after your exile was carefully destroyed by the unstoppable Platonic culture following your era.

"Because we accidentally 'saved' you, in conjunction with how my son is changing the way my machine interfaces with the people of my time, your work is now a part of their mental activity as if you'd never been lost to time."

"Your visit is not social," the philosopher said plainly.

"Though I am thrilled at the changes and was tempted to amplify and extend their reach, you are once again correct, we are not allowed to mess with our fellow citizens this way," Brink said, pained.

"Of course not. There is only one solution."

"Not exactly," Brink said as she watched Protagoras throw himself over the side of the cliff he deftly walked them to. "WAIT!" she cried as she raced to save him. It was far too late. The old man was no longer a part of the sim, his body contorted on the rocks below.

Brink was disgusted with the thought that popped into her head immediately — "If only I could autopsy that brain."

27 – THE SHOW MUST …

Sulis couldn't stop offering meals and drinks to everyone at the bar. She felt that celebrations weren't only warranted, but involuntary. Connectomes were bounding back at a possibly dangerous pace, but nonetheless perfectly. She wasn't sure Leopold would be interested in the story of the world's first mind bomb, mainly because he looked like he'd just come home from a war. He also hated the whole Citheron experience, being dragged off earth, shoved into a remote IMAC just to be returned to a fake Earth. Leopold never got into gaming, for a reason. He did enjoy the looks he got from Sulis for what he assumed was his ancient Greek SCkin. Leopold tried out his sexiest low ancient Greek voice. Sulis fell off her seat laughing. Leopold wasn't nearly as sensitive as he used to be, but his crushed expression made Sulis laugh a little more. She took his hand.

"My big man, why don't you tell me what happened. You look exhausted. Shall we go nap. I haven't slept in a couple days myself," Sulis said hoping to calm down from her exhausting internal celebrations.

"I know it's like cliche or something but I never worried in there because of you. I mean, thinking of you reminded me I wasn't really in danger. I'm not saying this right."

"You are saying it just right," Sulis said, kissing Leopold. He didn't even recoil as normally public displays of affection made him his version of nauseous.

"You're not going to believe this, but after all that, I want to make sure that we accomplish the mission we set out to do."

"She would be so proud to hear you say that."

"Yeah, I don't care about that. Do you know where Taer is? Did she arrive in Vancouver yet?"

"Wow, you're serious. Well, let's get this done. I think it's time we checked in on the boss in person as well."

Brink was not expecting to see grandma interact with Monkeybot first thing after decoupling from the IMAC.

The living room was full of folks, as planned, but it still felt shocking. Brink wandered past everyone on the way to a well-earned shower.

"Did someone build this to mock and torture you, because I love it too much," shouted Taer.

"Eat shit, mom," Brink bleated through a smile.

Taer followed after Brink and within earshot asked, "Why did you kidnap me?"

"You know why. And please don't say that. I had a real bad day at work."

"I'm way too old to give a shit about birthdays, so let's just have dinner then send me home."

"I love seeing you too even though you look terrible. When did you start looking old?"

"Try lookin in a mirror, ya wrinkly gorilla," said Monkeybot trailing behind them.

"I'm taking this robot home with me," said Taer.

163

"Try it and get zapped, crone of the dark night!"

"Did you program it like this because you missed me?"

"I do miss you," said Brink. "Now go sit down with your friends and the nerds I invited and take a bunch of deep breaths, because your surprise birthday gift is gonna fill your adult diapers."

"I knew those were diapers. Who could possibly have an ass shaped like that?!"

"I'm dating you now, robot. Can I ride those arms back to the ball room?"

"I'm not being suckered into falling into your cow parts, woman! Follow me, if you can."

Monkeybot sped back down the hall towards the party.

Brink took her time as the warm water blasted her weak and lonely muscles. She was nervous the sound of the high pressure shower would hide the arrival of her son from orbit. It did not. Prudence shook in that way Brink rarely got to experience. She was normally the one either piloting or riding along in the spacecopter. It sounded like Glas was trying to show off but came in too fast and had to land elsewhere. Adorable buffoon, thought Brink.

"Talk about someone I miss," Brink said to herself. "Let's get this party over with!"

She pranced to one of her many walk-in wardrobes and grabbed something comfy and revealing. Her usual.

"Grandma!" Leopold shouted as he ran towards an already half-asleep Taer.

Opening one eye, she quickly lifted herself up and cried, "wow, is this my beautiful lil boy?"

Leopold was always grossed out when he wore an objectively handsome SCkin and grandma noticed. But he was thrilled to see her anyway and gave her a choking hug.

"Oh if only Brink were here to witness this betrayal," said Monkeybot to a round of laughter, which of course made him shudder with pride.

"Do NOT encourage him, please!!" Brink cried as she walked in on the scene.

"Brink!" Leopold screamed, the sound like a cub finding his mother during a snowstorm. Leopold raced towards his mother and leapt into her outstretched arms. She was more than strong enough to hoist a teenage young man, but she put him down right away before the crowd erupted in awws. Though maybe Leopold had grown or changed a little and that level of attention and emotion didn't bother him as much anymore.

"You forgot to kiss your only son, Mrs. Wormwood!" Monkeybot screeched at Brink, once again to a round of laughter.

Leopold then leapt over to Monkeybot and hugged him.

"I thought I'd never see you again, old friend. Our mom tried to kill me in there!"

"My darling brother, I knew she would. I am so happy to have you back. You are my only friend."

"What about the coffee machine?"

"I hate her now!"

Leopold gave Monkeybot a kiss on the nose, then the silly little radio array on the top of his head. Monkeybot cooed.

Brink wandered in front of her wall-sized windows and addressed everyone in the room, "I am extremely sorry we are so late and that the surprise part of my mom's 100th birthday was ruined. But this is all quite auspicious because we got the problems out of the way and this time, what I ruined so long ago should come off without a hitch."

"Don't be a dick. Grandma is 60. You're turning 60, right?" Leopold said.

Taer blew a kiss at her adoring grandson, extra proud that he seemed to finally be standing up to his mother.

"The original plan here was to shove you all in the IMAC, and do not stress, that will still be available to all the esteemed scholars in the room, as usual. But it is this mad woman's 60th birthday and I will do the best I can to give her this long overdue gift. Are we all ready to put on some IMAC headsets?

Taer couldn't figure out whether she was more confused about what Brink was talking about or that everyone else seemed to understand completely.

Sulis, Duana, Glas, and Brink helped Monkeybot distribute large domed helmets.

"They just sit on your head any way you find comfy. If they feel weird, or if you are just now realizing you are claustrophobic, I have glasses. The helmets give you more senses. Nothing like being IN the IMAC, but trust me, you'll freak out. In a good way."

Leopold helped Taer, both of them knowing he was the only one she'd trust to hook her into anything.

"Wait till I tell you the fucking crazy stuff we went through to get this," Leopold said.

"We're saying fuck now?!" Taer said, giggling, the echo freaking her out, in a neutral way.

"Yeah, well the story will justify that, trust me."

"I can't wait. Let's go do that now. What is this shit?"

"You are going to love it. I promise. Try to breathe normal and let it flow. It's cool. I love interfacing this way."

"Thank you, sweetie. I love you."

"I bet she never said that to you!" Monkeybot said to Brink.

"I love you too, apebot," Taer said.

"Eat shit, mom! My name is Monkeybot," he said, gliding past. "Enjoy the show!"

And with that, Brink dimmed the lights and started the replay.

It took the scholars in the audience seconds before they gasped and shook with glee, recognizing where they were instantly. Taer sat confused but engaged and curious. Those feelings were obliterated within moments when she read the titles under the ancient Greek dialog.

> If they were trysting for a Bacchanal,
> A feast of Pan or Colias or Genetyllis,
> The tambourines would block the rowdy streets,
> But now there's not a woman to be seen
> Except — ah, yes — this neighbor of mine yonder.
> Calonice. Good day Calonice.

Taer started having trouble breathing. Brink had been keeping a close eye on her and spoke gently though Taer's helmet's speaker, "Taer, it's okay... keep breathing. This is exactly what you think it is. Enjoy it, okay. I owed you one."

Taer began sobbing. She could neither hear nor see anything but her own rapturous happiness.

Brink hit pause and approached Taer circuitously so it wasn't obvious what she was up to.

"One moment everyone. Technical difficulties," Brink told the room.

"Old age difficulties," added Monkeybot.

Taer got it together, she was desperate to. She hadn't figured out yet, why would she, that she was watching the very first performance of Lysistrata. That would have killed her, thought Brink. Taer even managed a laugh, several, when she noticed that all the actors were men. The crying never really stopped though. She was too proud, too amazed, and too honored to be in any way relaxed while witnessing this miracle.

It did cross Brink's mind to interrupt the play just when she had as a kid as a joke, but she had no memory of what part of the play that was exactly. She was thrilled to see Leopold watching too. He didn't look traumatized at all. This thought made Brink laugh, which turned her attention to Monkeybot staring at something behind the audience. It was Glas. Brink had completely forgotten another hero of the day.

Glas waved her over with the muscles of his neck and a head toss. Brink got a little weak-kneed. She tried to indicate that she had to keep an eye on Taer and the projection, and everyone really. Glas made some obscene gestures and tried to indicate that it would be real quick. Brink twirled her finger in a way to indicate "go behind the bar and get on the floor." It seemed to work.

Brink moved as stealthily as she was able, checking helmets as she went and making sure neither Taer nor Leopold paid any attention to her movements. When she reached the bar, she pretended to pour a drink in case anyone was looking, then snuck quickly around to a delightfully erect and unclothed Glas.

"Dr. Brink Shelby, this is a special unit of the ICC. Your home is surrounded," came the words from an amped-up bullhorn. "Please come out what we assume is your front door with your arms above your head. You have six minutes to comply."

"You have to be joking," Brink growled to herself.

"Honey, you have to deal with this. It's okay," Glas said, forgetting who he was talking to.

"It is not okay," Brink commanded. "The only reason I am not riding you for about five minutes is because this is a hilarious situation." Brink stood and marched towards the audience. Looking at Taer's childlike joy was too much; she changed plans and marched out her front door.

Leopold shut down the immersion.

"I am really sorry everyone," said Leopold to the audience. Taer looked confused and worried as she watched Leopold speedily float after Brink. Monkeybot had whispered to him, "Hey, I think your mom's getting arrested."

Made in the USA
Monee, IL
18 January 2026